Don't Judge a Book by Its Cover

Susan Potter

Write For Life Publishing —Tonawanda, NY
ISBN: 978-0-578-50014-0
Library of Congress Control Number: 2019904963
Available Formats: eBook | Paperback

Dedication

I would like to dedicate this book to my
grandchildren:
Cameron, Carter, Cohen, Annabelle, Evelyn,
Hunter, and Lennon
May you stand tall in who you are, and live your
lives with kindness
to yourselves and to others.
I would also like to dedicate my book to all those
who have been on either side of the bully fence.
I wish for you the peace and direction to
knowing you are loved and loveable.
Always remember… You are a beautiful child of
God!

Chapter One

Yea! It's summer vacation! Ruby couldn't wait to get home to meet her new neighbors. She heard that there was a kid her age moving in and she was so glad! She had been the only kid in the neighborhood for as long as she could remember and she was done being lonely. Ruby got on her shiny red bike and raced home in time to see the moving trucks pulling up. She parked her bike in the garage and went inside to see what her mom had out for a snack for her. She hoped it was something she could eat on the front porch so she could spy a little bit before going over to introduce herself to her new friend. She couldn't wait! She hoped she would like to play games and have lots of stuffed animals they could play with and share.

As Ruby sat on her front porch eating her cookies and drinking her milk, she scoped out the new neighbor's house and what was being taken in by the movers. So far, she hadn't seen anything of the new neighbors. They must be inside directing the movers as to where to put things. Lots of boxes! So many boxes! She wasn't seeing any toys or a bike or anything kid related being taken off the truck and started to fret that maybe it was a mistake and no kid would be moving in after all. Ohhh, she hoped there was and the kid would be her age! Suddenly a big furry dog came bounding out the front door! It was brown and big, well at least it looked big to her! Did Ruby like dogs? Well, she never really was around them but she was about to find out how she felt about them as it ran across the lawns and up to her front steps to lick her and jump on her. She started to laugh as he was tickling her face with wet kisses! Next came a boy running after his dog calling his name…

"Rangerrrrr!"

Then she realized her new friend was a boy…. a little disappointment, but she'd take it, a new friend! "Ranger, come here!" he shouted as he stopped short noticing Ruby sitting with his dog, he looked embarrassed.

Hector was unsure of meeting someone so soon; his dad got a new job, so they were moving into a nicer, bigger house in a new neighborhood. I guess Ranger thought it was the perfect time to meet his new neighbor. He slowed down as he got closer to the porch, he was out of breath from the short run. Hector was not used to a lot of exercise. He saw Ruby stand up and he didn't know what to think. Was she going to tell him to take his dog and get lost? He felt himself get ready for the rejection. But nope, instead she stood to welcome him.

"Hi! I'm Ruby, your new neighbor! Nice dog!" as she hugged his neck and petted his back.

Hector was at a loss for words and so he stuttered, "Ha ha ha hi. I'm Heh heh Hector. I'm ss so sorry I I if my d dddog b b b bothered you."

Oh boy, thought Ruby, how could she have a new friend that couldn't even talk right? Ruby looked him over and noticed that his appearance was not so good either. His clothes for one thing were too small for him and his belly was sticking out. But he did have red sneakers on and a red shirt, and it was her favorite color. Her mind seemed to be arguing about this new friend but even though her first impression was not good, her heart wanted to give him a chance and it's not like she had many choices since she was the only kid in her neighborhood. All her playdates had to be thought out and arranged by parents. She asked him to have a seat on the porch and she went inside to see if her mom would be ok with her sharing some more cookies and milk with her new friend and neighbor.

"Moooom! Our new neighbor is here and I'd like to share my snack with him! Can you give me more cookies and a glass of milk for him? His name is Hector and he has a dog named Ranger. Hurry mom, before he leaves!" Ruby had a habit of running all her words together in such a hurry to get them out and her mom had to remind her all the time to slow it down so she could understand what she was saying and have time to reply.

"Slow down missy prissy! Let's go meet this new friend of yours!" So together they went out to the porch and Ruby introduced her mom to Hector. Ranger introduced himself with a big lick and by wagging his tale so hard it almost knocked over Ruby's milk. Before Ruby's mom would invite Hector to stay for cookies and milk, she insisted he go home and let his mom know where he was.

Soon Hector was back with Ranger trailing alongside him. Ruby's mom brought out more cookies and milk and left them to get acquainted. Suddenly Ruby was shy too; she didn't know how to start this friendship so it was quiet as they both munched on their cookies. She kept sneaking a peak at him. In her mind she was not liking what she saw. He was sloppy and fat. But some part of her felt like she needed to give him a chance, so she jumped in with some questions for him. "So, Hector, how old are you? What grade are you in? Where did you live before?" Then she realized that she wasn't giving him a chance to answer one question before she asked another, especially since he didn't talk too good when he first came over. So, she stopped and waited.

Hector hesitated, trying to calm down his inner fears of saying something that would not be right. He didn't want to ruin this chance at having a new friend. He was always so lonely and didn't have many friends at his old house. He didn't want to stutter so he started out slowly.

"I I I'm 12 years old." He hesitated again and Ruby felt herself getting agitated while at the same time she feeling sorry for him. He was not living up to her expectation of this new friend.

"I I I'm in 6th grade and we lived in Tonawanda be be before we m m moved here." Hector was feeling angry at himself for not being able to answer a simple question without stuttering. He wanted to get up and run home to his new room and stay there forever with his dog! Ruby looked just like one of the popular kids and he knew it was just a matter of time before she started to make fun of him or just ignore him.

Ruby was a popular kid but not one that had to make fun of others to have her peers look up to her. Ruby was her own person who talked to everyone and everyone talked to her. Hector wondered how that happened. Who decided who was popular or better than others? What was he missing in his person that made him so undesirable? He struggled with those questions a lot.

As the afternoon wore on, Ruby and Hector got to know one another better and seemed to be getting along. Hector relaxed a little and was not stuttering as much and the funny thing was that now Ruby didn't seem to mind his stuttering. In the back of his mind though he was dreading the time when Ruby would realize that he was not worth her time and would start ignoring him like all the others had.

Soon the movers were closing up to leave. All the furniture and boxes were inside the house now and it was time to start settling in. Hector and Ranger headed home across the yards to help set up his room.

Chapter Two

Ruby woke up to the first day of summer vacation with hopes of spending time with her new friend and getting to know him better. She raced down the stairs to breakfast thinking she would quickly eat and then go over to Hectors to meet his mom and start the friendship. Her mom had other ideas for her start to summer vacation. Ruby would have a list of chores to do each day before she got to do what she wanted to do. First off was making her bed and straightening up her room. Ruby had a habit of just leaving things lying wherever she finished using them and now she would be responsible to clean up after herself. Bummer! She also had to take her bowl from the table and put it into the dishwasher, brush her teeth and fix her hair. She had to do these things during the school year, and she thought since it was summer vacation, she would take a vacation from being responsible too. Ugh...being twelve is almost like being an adult!

Hector woke up to the fist morning in his new home. He stretched out in his bed and thought about his new friend and if they would spend the day together and what they would do. His room was coming along good. His bed was up and his dresser with all his clothes was in place. He didn't tell too many people but he loved stuffed animals and so he had a little display of them on the bench near the window. He didn't play with them as much as love them. Ranger slept on his bed with him and he was also stretching probably looking forward to a day of exploring his new surroundings. There was a wooded area with a little pond behind the house that Hector was excited to explore and he knew that Ranger would love it too.

Hector scrambled down the stairs to the kitchen where his mom was putting away dishes and arranging things. She had to find him a bowl so he could have his bowl of Frosted Flakes. He felt like he was looking forward to the day, but also afraid of what it would bring. He had hopes that he and Ruby would become good friends. Hector thought he'd eat and be out the door to meet up with Ruby, but his mom needed his help for a while so he slowed down and enjoyed his breakfast. He was looking forward to setting up his Play Station in the family room and wondered if Ruby liked to play Pac Man too.

After lunch Hector's mom told him he could go explore for a while before dinner time so he and Ranger headed out towards Ruby's house to see if she could play and at the same time she was headed out her door to see if he could play. She thought she would show him the wooded area behind their houses and maybe he would like searching for critters and exploring like she did. She had her red rain boots on so that she didn't have to worry about getting in the mud at the edge of the pond. When they met up and she asked him if he'd like to join her, he felt pretty excited. They went back to his house to search for his boots and Ruby got to meet his mom, who she thought was very nice. His stuttering was starting to be less and less as the day went on. They each had a bucket to collect Crayfish and whatever other critters they could find. Ruby's first impressions were starting to fade. She was no longer looking at him thinking he was sloppy or fat and his nervous stutter was not so much. She saw him as a friend… *This might work,* she thought! Suddenly Ruby heard the dinner bell. Her mom was calling her to dinner already. The afternoon went so fast! Time flies when you're having fun!

After dinner Hector had to stay home and help his mom and dad get settled in their new house. Hector's dad was going to set up the family room and that meant his video games would be up and running in no time! Ruby also had to stay home to spend some time with her mom and dad. Her mom popped some popcorn and they played UNO and Monopoly till bed time. As Ruby got into bed, she was feeling very happy about how the day went. She had such a good time with Hector and looked forward to tomorrow when they would go back to the woods and the pond to play. Hector and Ranger were also very tired out and grateful for the day when they hopped into bed at the end of that first day of summer vacation. *I think it's going to be a nice summer,* Hector thought as he closed his eyes to dream about the next day with his new friend.

Chapter Three

The next morning after Ruby's chores were done, her mom surprised her with two lunches packed, one for her and one for Hector. Ruby put them in her back pack and grabbed a couple of fishing poles and headed over to Hector's to see if he could spend the day exploring and having a picnic with her. Hector's mom was ok with it so Hector packed some treats for Ranger and the three of them set out for the woods. Oh, what a nice day it was! The sun was shining and it wasn't too hot. They chatted on the way there, becoming more comfortable with each other all the time. Hector's stutter seemed to be gone.

They found a good spot to set up for the day and Ruby brought out the fishing poles. Hector looked a little frightened. He never fished and was afraid he wouldn't do it right and embarrass himself. *This is it*, he thought, *I'm going to mess up this friendship now; she's going to hate me.* Ruby noticed that he looked a little fearful and so she reassured him that she would teach him to fish and he would love it.

First, they had to find some bait. So together they started lifting rocks looking for a few big worms. It was a lot of fun and Hector almost forgot what they were getting the worms for, until it was time to put them on the hook. He watched Ruby thread a worm on the hook. Oh my gosh! He felt sorry for the worm! How could she do that?? Didn't that hurt? How was he going to get out of this? He started to get a stomach ache! Oh no!

"I I I'll wa wa watch you fi fi fi fish Ruby, I dddon't need to do it," Hector stammered. Ugh, now the stuttering was back! He was failing fishing and they hadn't even started yet!

Suddenly Ranger started barking and running back and forth. What could he be barking at? Could he be feeling sorry for the worm too? Was there someone out there in the woods? Ruby set the worm and hook down and her and Hector froze for a few moments wondering what could be out there. *Someone has to take charge here,* thought Ruby. Since Ranger was Hector's dog, she looked to him. Nope. I guess it would be her job, Hector was not moving. He looked terrified. Ruby called out to Ranger, but he did not come, he just kept barking and pacing back and forth. Ruby stepped forward to see if she could see what was there and here came a mommy duck and six little ducklings walking as calm as could be towards the water. The ducks did not seem bothered at all with all the commotion of the barking pacing dog. Ruby started to laugh and encouraged Hector to come look. She didn't tell him what she saw, and so he was still afraid.

"Hector, Hector, come look! Don't be afraid, come look!" Ruby whispered loudly.

Hector stepped forward to see what he could see. A slow smile started to appear on his face and then he was laughing too! They finally got Ranger to stop barking by giving him some treats and they all sat down to watch the ducks waddle into the water and start swimming around. As they sat there, Hector hoped that Ruby forgot about the worms and the fishing, but after they watched for a little while, she was back at it, telling him it was his turn to thread the worm on the hook. Hector did not want to let her down so he picked up the slimy worm and the hook but he just couldn't do it. He was close to tears because he wanted so badly to do it, but he knew he would not do this. He set it down and just hung his head in shame. Ruby remembered the first time she went fishing with her dad and it was time for her to put the worm on the hook. She too was not able to do it, so she took the hook and the worm and did it for him. Hector was amazed. He thought for sure she would send him home or just make fun of him, but she was so nice to him. Hector was also grossed out but he managed to hide that from Ruby. Instead he acted grateful and then they were ready to fish! She explained how to toss the line in the water and wait for the tug on the line which meant a fish was nibbling on the worm.

They sat at the edge of the pond and waited. They talked and laughed and just had a good time together. Suddenly there was a tugging on Hector's line. He wasn't sure what to do, but he was excited!

"Ruby, Ruby! Help Me!" Hector shouted.

Ruby set her pole down and coached him till he brought his fish in. It was a Sunfish and a big one too! Hector was excited; he never had so much fun!

"What do we do with it? What do we do with it?" Hector asked.

Ruby held the fish up and told him he had to take the hook out of its mouth and then they would throw it back in the water, they were only fishing for fun. Hector suddenly realized that the fish had that hook in its mouth and the worm was gone. Hector has a very soft heart. He can't stand to see animals hurt and now look what he did. He was almost in tears and Ruby wasn't sure what was going on, so she asked him what was wrong. He didn't answer so she said to him,

"Don't worry Hector, I'll take the fish off the hook for you, it's ok." And so Ruby took the hook out and asked Hector if he wanted to release the fish back into the water.

Hector gently took the fish from Ruby and walked to the edge of the pond. He bent down to let the fish go and whoops he slipped in the mud! Bam! The fish went flying into the air before landing in the water to swim away. Hector ended up on his butt in the water too! Ruby was laughing so hard…he looked so funny sitting in the water, mud all over him including his face. Hector got mad. He thought she was making fun of him. He tried to get up and fell again which made Ruby laugh even harder. Finally, he crawled to drier land and got up and just started walking away with his head down. He was covered in mud. Ruby realized that he was mad or his feelings were hurt, she wasn't sure which so she ran after him. He wouldn't look up. He had so many feelings going on. He was embarrassed, and hurt that she laughed, and mad that she might have been making fun of him, he just wanted to go home.

"Hector, Hector, I'm sorry I laughed! You just looked so funny, I'm sorry, please stop and talk to me!"

Hector didn't say anything and kept walking; he didn't want her to see that he was crying. So, Ruby let him go. Ranger was staying right with him as he walked home with his best friend. Ruby went back to their site and started to clean up. She was very upset and didn't know what to do to make this ok. She packed up her backpack and went home. She too was crying by the time she got there.

"Mom!" She cried out. "Mom!" Her mom came from the basement. She was doing laundry.

"What's wrong honey? Where's Hector?" Ruby started to cry harder and her mom came to her and put an arm around her to lead her to the couch where they could talk about what was going on.

Chapter Four

Ruby's words tumbled out so fast that her mom could barely understand what she was saying.

"Slow down, honey.... just take a breath and tell me what happened, is Hector ok?" her mom asked.

After Ruby calmed enough to tell her mom the story, her mom suggested they go over to Hectors and talk to him and his mom and see if they could get this misunderstanding taken care of. Ruby wasn't sure that would help, Hector was so upset; she thought she lost her new friend for good. *Oh, why did I laugh? Well because he looked so funny, I wasn't making fun of him* she thought. She was afraid Hector's mom would be mad at her too, she was afraid to go over there. Ruby felt so bad for so many things. She felt bad that Hector fell in the mud, she felt bad for laughing at Hector and she felt bad that she didn't know how to make it better. She just felt bad bad bad!

After Ruby washed her face and calmed down, her and her mom walked over to the new neighbors. Ruby was nervous and afraid. She didn't mean to hurt Hector; she didn't mean to be mean either. She hoped he would forgive her. Hector's mom and a barking Ranger came to the door when they knocked. She had an apron on and the aroma of chocolate chip cookies came through the screen door. *Mmmm,* thought Ruby almost forgetting why they were there. Ruby's mom introduced herself and Hector's mom did the same as she invited them inside. Ranger was friendly as ever, but eventually laid down on his dog bed with a toy he was trying to destroy. Hector was nowhere to be seen. Hector's mom showed them to the kitchen where they sat at a big kitchen table. It smelled so good in there. Ruby's mom started out the conversation.

"It seems that Ruby might have hurt Hector's feeling this morning and we came over to talk about it. Ruby has been very upset and she wanted Hector to know how very sorry she is that she laughed when he fell in the mud."

Hector's mom excused herself and left the room. Ruby and her mom didn't know what to think. A few minutes later she was back with a cleaned up Hector. He stood with his head down and his hands at his sides not saying anything. He looked so beaten down. Ruby felt even worse when she saw him.

Hector's mom said, "Hector, Ruby came over to tell you something, have a seat honey."

Hector obediently slunk into the chair; head still down, arms hanging. He looked so ashamed and sad. For a minute Ruby could not speak, which is unusual for her. She was choked up, feeling like she might cry for him.

And then she said, "Hector, I'm so sorry I hurt your feelings. It's just that you looked so funny sitting there in the mud. I wasn't laughing at you to be mean, honest."

Slowly Hector lifted his head. She could tell he had been crying because his eyes were red. He didn't know how to respond. No one ever apologized to him before. He wanted to forgive her, but didn't know how to tell her that. What words do you use to forgive someone for hurting your feelings? Should he say, ok thanks? Or, don't worry about it? Or should he deny that she hurt his feelings in the first place? His mom put her arm around the back of him. It was really quiet for a moment while Hector struggled with what to say.

His mom broke the silence, she said, "It was so nice of Ruby to come over to tell you how sorry she is, Hector. Would you like to say anything to her in return?"

Hector just didn't know what to say, so he said nothing, just kept his head down.

Finally, he looked up at Ruby and just said, "Thank you."

And Ruby smiled big. Hector started to explain that he was also upset because he felt bad for the worm and for the fish. He did not want to hurt them. Ruby felt like her heart had been touched by love. Hector was really a nice guy! He had feelings that hurt him and she wanted to make sure she would not hurt him again. He had feelings for all living things. This was a friend she wanted to keep!

Hector's mom got up and gathered the cookies she just took out of the oven. She poured two glasses of milk and two cups of coffee and the four of them shared this little snack in the middle of the day. Hector's mom and Ruby's mom started to talk about mom stuff and so Ruby and Hector finished up their cookies and milk and scooted off to the family room. It turned out that Ruby loved to play Pac Man and so that is how they finished out their day together. Friends once again.

Chapter Five

The next day it was raining. Ruby was bored and so was Hector. Both just sitting in their rooms staring out at the rain coming down with thunder and lightning. Ranger was under the bed. Ruby's mom suggested she call Hector and invite him over to play some board games and video games too. So, she did and a half hour later, Hector was at her door under an umbrella with his favorite card game and his Rubik's Cube. Ruby never knew anyone who could solve a Rubik's Cube so she was curious to see it happen. She invited him in and started to lead him to her room. Her mom stopped them and told them they could play in the family room or in the basement, not in her bedroom. They both did not understand so her mom explained that bedrooms were private places and boys did not go in girl's bedrooms and girls did not go in boy's bedrooms. Ruby was disappointed because she wanted to show him her stuffed animal collection, but they turned around and went into the family room without a fight. She would just have to bring out her favorites to show him.

They played UNO for a while before Ruby was anxious to see Hector solve the Rubik's Cube. He had her mix it up for him so she wouldn't think he cheated. Within a minute he had it solved! She was so impressed! He tried to teach her but she couldn't understand about the algorithms so she gave up and left that talent for him. She mixed it up a few more times for him before her mom came in with some fruit for a treat. After their treat, Ruby asked Hector if he wanted to see some of her stuffed animals. She thought he would say no thanks since he was a boy, but he seemed real interested so she went to her room and scooped up a few of her favorites. Hector confided in her that he loved stuffed animals and had quite a few himself and promised to show her his when she came to his house. They played a little bit with the stuffed animals and told each other which ones were their favorite and why. Ruby started to think that it was a little odd that a boy would like stuffed animals but then let it go…. who cares? And why not like stuffed animals? They're pretty cool! Hector's mom called and it was time for Hector to go home. The rain had not let up at all so Hector put up his umbrella and headed out into the rain for his walk across the lawns.

After Hector left, Ruby thought she would call one of her friends to chat on the phone for a while. So, she called Andrea who lived on the other side of town. Ruby was telling her about her new friend and how much fun they have together. Andrea asked her if he was her boyfriend.

"Well," said Ruby, "he is a boy and he's my friend, but he's not my boyfriend."

"What's the difference?" Andrea asked.

Ruby wasn't sure, but she knew there was a difference. Andrea started to tease her and sing,

"Ruby's got a boyfriend; Ruby's got a boyfriend."

Ruby was getting mad, but she felt confused at the same time. Was he her boyfriend? What is the difference? When she got off the phone she went to find her mom to ask her this question.

"Mooom..." she whined, "Andrea says that Hector is my boyfriend! Is he?"

Her mom hmmm-ed, then she sighed while she thought over how to answer this question.

"Well," she said. "Hector is a boy and he is your friend, so he is a boy friend, but he's a friend just like Andrea is a girl friend to you. A boyfriend is a boy that you have deeper feelings for, different feelings that you will understand when you get a little bit older and learn about romance, but for now you're too young to worry about that, just enjoy your friendship and don't worry what others think."

Ruby always felt better when she talked things over with her mom, but this time she still felt confused and wasn't sure what to do with that confusion. She thought she might invite Andrea over sometime to play together with Hector so she could see what a good friend he could be.

Chapter Six

Ruby and Hector continued to enjoy each other's company and summer vacation. Hector never had such a good friend. His mom bought him a bike and him and Ruby rode bikes and explored in the woods and just had a good time together. Ruby asked her mom if her friend Andrea could come over to meet Hector and play together and so they made a sleep over date. Ruby was so excited, she told Hector about it and he got really quiet. He could feel the dread seeping into his mind. He and Ruby were good friends, he never had a friend like her and he was afraid he would lose her when Andrea joined their fun. He tried to look excited, but Ruby felt his fear. She wasn't sure what to do about it so she just let it pass thinking everything would be ok once he met Andrea.

It was finally Friday and Andrea would be coming to Ruby's house in about a half hour. Ruby was getting her room ready for the sleep over. She had her sleeping bag out and her favorite stuffed animals surrounding it. She left a space for Andrea's sleeping bag and her stuffed animals. She had her nail polish out so they could paint each other's nails after a day of playing in the woods with Hector.

Hector was at home wondering what the day was going to be like. He was dreading Andrea's visit. He feared it would be the end of his friendship with Ruby. I mean, Ruby was like a miracle. She liked him. She didn't mind if he stuttered sometimes or didn't want to fish, and she didn't care that he was so fat and unlikeable. He couldn't figure out why she liked him but he liked it, he liked having a friend. What if Andrea didn't like him like most kids? Would she make Ruby not like him? It was bound to happen sooner or later because when school started he was sure Ruby would go her own way with her own friends and he would be back to the loneliness of having no one to laugh with or play Pac Man with or explore the woods.

"Andrea's here!!" shouted Ruby.

Andrea's mom helped her to carry all her stuff into the house. She had her sleeping bag and her bag of clothes and of course her stuffed animals. She also brought a couple of movies in case they had time to watch them. Andrea and Ruby's mom talked for a little while and Ruby and Andrea set up their sleeping area. Everything had to be just right. Ruby was excited to introduce her friend to her new friend. Andrea however, would have rather had Ruby all to herself. They hadn't been together in quite a while. Plus, it was a boy. Why would Ruby want to be friends with a boy, was it her boyfriend? Ugh!

Hector paced the floor in his room waiting for Ruby and Andrea to come over. Ruby said they would be over after lunch. Suddenly he heard the knock at the door and Ranger was barking. His mom answered the door and called out to Hector. Slowly Hector walked out of his room to what he thought was his doom.

"Hi Hector!" said Ruby.

Hector said hello and then Ruby introduced Andrea. Hector said hello and got all shy, he was afraid he would start stuttering if he said too much. He stood there with his head down and shuffled his feet. Andrea looked him over. This was the new friend? Hector could see the disgust on Andrea's face. Ruby did not notice what was going on; she was just excited to have her two friends together.

"Come on, let's go play!" Ruby said.

Hector followed them out the door. Andrea just couldn't get over this new friend of Ruby's, I mean look at him…. he's fat and his clothes are so uncool. His hair is a mess and he doesn't even talk very well, and this dog! Ranger was excited to have a new person and was jumping up on her trying to get a lick in, but Andrea was having none of that. She kept pushing him down and Ruby told her he only did that if he liked you, and that did not comfort Andrea, she didn't like dogs.

Off they went to the woods. Hector trailed behind them while Ranger ran up front. Hector thought his dog was a traitor and wished he would come back and walk with him.

Andrea was whispering to Ruby, "What the heck, Ruby...this kid is weird!"

Ruby felt defensive but did not defend Hector. She thought once they got to the woods and started playing; Andrea would see what a good friend Hector could be. She remembered what she thought when she first met him and how all that went away when she got to know him. So, she just had to give it a chance, but she felt bad for Hector.

Hector heard the whisper. He sunk further into himself with fear and humiliation. He wanted to go home to his room and be alone. But he trudged along behind them for Ruby. When they got to the woods Ruby decided they would play on the tire swing. Andrea thought for sure that if Hector took a turn, he would snap the rope. Ruby thought nothing of it when she took her turn and then held the tire out for Hector.

Andrea said, "Are you sure that rope will hold him?"

She had a real sneer on her face when she said it. It sounded mean and Ruby heard it. What should she do? What should she say? How could she make this better? Hector was a good friend, why won't Andrea give him a chance? She just wanted her two friends to like each other and Andrea was not off to a good start. She could see Hector feeling the hurt, but she still didn't say anything. What could she say? This was going to be a long afternoon. Maybe it was a mistake to do this.

"Let's just take a hike," Ruby said, trying to avoid what was obviously getting worse by the minute.

They started out on a trail. Ruby and Hector loved the trails and all the critters and bugs and birds they would see along the way. Andrea did not like the hike. She hated bugs and was afraid of critters. Birds? She could care less about them as long as they didn't poop on her head. Ruby decided that they should just go back to her house and play some games. On the way back, Hector told Ruby that he wasn't feeling well and was going home. Ruby felt so bad but didn't know how to make it better. She let him go.

Hector felt so bad on his way home. He couldn't wait to get to his room, but he also was so disappointed in Ruby. She already went her own way back to her own friends and they weren't even in school yet. How could he have thought that their friendship was real? Hector stayed in his room all afternoon till his mom called him out for dinner. He wasn't really hungry and his mom knew something must have happened in the woods with Ruby and Andrea but Hector was not talking. Hector's mom knew in her heart that Hector must be feeling left out. She knew he got bullied a lot in school, but this summer had been so good for him with Ruby as his friend. She loved her little boy and couldn't figure out why others were not as crazy about him as she was. It made her heart ache.

Ruby and Andrea went back to Ruby's house. Ruby could not stop thinking about Hector and how he must be feeling, but Andrea didn't want to talk about him, she was glad he was gone. So Ruby and Andrea spent the rest of the afternoon in her room painting each other's nails. Ruby's dad came home from work and decided to grill out. He asked Ruby if she wanted to invite the new neighbors. She had to think about that, and she even felt bad about having to think about it, but she didn't want to further hurt Hector. Her mom heard the invitation and told Ruby she thought that would be a good idea so Ruby made the phone call. Hector would not come to the phone so she gave the invite to his mom who said they would be happy to come and she would bring some dessert. Ruby had a nervous stomach after that. Should she talk to Andrea about her behavior? Should she speak up for Hector? She wanted them both to be her friend but how could that happen. Would she have to pick which one she liked better?

Chapter Seven

Ruby really wanted to talk to her mom, but how could she with Andrea here? She was starting to get a stomach ache, so she told Andrea she would be right back and went in search of her mom. She found her in the basement doing the laundry. She was glad to find her down there for a private talk.

"Mom," she said, "I'm not sure what to do. I have two friends that don't like each other. One is getting hurt feelings because of the other one. What do I do? How can I make this better? How do I know which one I like better?"

Ruby's mom sat her down and asked her what was going on. She told her all about when she first met Hector and how she thought about him and how she got to know him and now she really likes him and wants him for a friend, but when she introduced Andrea to him, Andrea didn't like him immediately and she didn't try to hide it. Ruby thought her friend was rude, but she didn't know what to do about it.

Ruby's mom had to think for a minute. This was a difficult situation.

"Well Ruby, this certainly is not easy. You do not have to pick the one you like better, you don't have to like one more than the other either. Maybe you could talk to Andrea and share what you shared with me, that you had those feelings at first too, but once you got to know him, you really liked him. It shouldn't matter what someone is wearing or how they look, everyone should be given a chance. And if you still don't like them, you don't have to make fun of them or be rude about it. You have to decide what kind of person you want to be." Ruby felt better but was still nervous about talking to Andrea.

When Ruby got upstairs, Andrea was wondering where Ruby was, so Ruby knew it was time to talk to her friend especially since Hector and his parents were coming for dinner and would be there soon.

"Andrea, we need to talk." Ruby said.

Andrea looked at her with confusion. They had been talking, so what was this new talk going to be about, it sounded serious but she really had no idea. They went back to Ruby's room and sat on the bed together. Ruby was unsure of how to start so she just jumped in,

"I want to talk about Hector," she said. "He is my friend, but when I first met him I had thoughts in my head that really were not nice. If

I would have let those thoughts stay and grow worse and worse, I would not have the friend I have in Hector now. I know he's fat and sloppy, I know he stutters when he gets nervous, and I know he's kind of quiet, but he's also someone who doesn't try to be someone he's not, he's very kind and loves all animals, and he will be a true friend. I think Hector was bullied in his old school and I hope that he will be treated nicer at our school. It would be nice for him to start out with two friends that know him and will stick up for him. I hope you will be one of those friends for him, because I know I will be there for him."

Andrea didn't know what to say. She felt guilty and didn't know how to act or be from here on in. Ruby just sat quietly and let her friend think about it. Ruby knew the kind of person she wanted to be, would Andrea want to be like that too? Before Andrea could say anything, the door bell rang and the neighbors were here so nothing was said but Ruby felt better for telling her friend how she felt. Andrea was hanging her head a little bit.

Down in the kitchen Ruby's mom was just putting the coffee on and setting out the paper plates for the cookout. Ruby loved cookouts but she was still a little nervous about Andrea and

Hector. Her dad went to the door to welcome the neighbors. It was the first time that he would meet Hector's dad. Hector looked a lot like his dad for sure. He had the same short blond hair and kind of on the bigger side. He too looked a little bit messy. Ruby looked to Andrea to see what her response would be, but Andrea seemed a little withdrawn and quiet. That did not make Ruby feel better about how things could turn out. She just wanted her two friends to like each other and get along good. The dads were shaking hands and introducing theirselves to each other when in came Ranger. Ruby's dad had heard about Ranger but never met him either. Her dad loved dogs and so he welcomed Ranger to the cookout. Ruby thought she saw Andrea roll her eyes, but she couldn't be sure. She hoped that Andrea would change her mind about Hector, but she kinda knew that she wouldn't change her mind about Ranger.

Everyone was out in the back yard enjoying the fellowship and the nice weather. The hot dogs sure did smell good, especially to Ranger! Andrea was keeping to herself. Hector and Ruby pulled out the Yatzee game and asked her if she wanted to play. She did not. She wanted to go home, so she went inside and called her mom to come get her. Ruby didn't know about it until Andrea's mom was at the door. She was surprised and hurt. She felt like she was losing her friend over another one. She looked to her mom who just nodded as if to say it was ok. Ruby helped Andrea gather her things and walked her to the door. Neither girl said anything to each other. Ruby was quite upset on the inside, but she didn't want to ruin the evening for everyone else so she smiled and went back to the Yatzee game. Hector felt like it was his fault that Andrea left. He felt like he did something wrong, but he followed Ruby's lead and settled into the Yatzee game. They were both pretty quiet though. Ruby couldn't wait till everybody left. She felt like a ticking time bomb on the edge of tears on the inside. It's really hard work to make it look like everything is ok when it's not.

Chapter Eight

Ruby was getting ready for bed when her mom came into her room. They both sat on the edge of the bed, Ruby hugging one of her stuffed animals. She started to cry and her mom hugged her and rubbed her back telling her it was going to be ok.

"Maybe Andrea needs to go home and think about what you shared with her," her mom said. "If she comes back as your friend then she's a real friend. You had to decide whether or not you wanted to be like a bully and you made that decision not to when you accepted Hector for who he is, not what he looks like, what others think of him, or what he seems like. I'm proud of you honey. Andrea will come around, and if she doesn't then maybe she was not a good friend for you to have. I love you so much Ruby."

Ruby started to feel a little better, but she was still hurting for both friends. She felt like she was stuck in the middle and it didn't feel good. She wondered what it was going to be like when school started up in September.

"I don't care what anyone thinks, Hector is a good friend to have!" Ruby said with a lot of uncertainty.

She had a hard time sleeping that night because it felt like she could not turn her mind off and when she did sleep, she dreamt of what school might be like this year. *It sure is hard to be 12 sometimes*, Ruby thought...but what she didn't know is that these kinds of situations didn't just happen to kids or 12-year old's, adults have this happen too. That's why it's good to decide what kind of person you want to be like when you are young. If your struggling with something like this, it usually means you really do know the right thing to do but you wonder or worry what others will think. Always do the right thing, you will feel better for it.

Hector laid in his bed thinking about the last two days. Meeting Ruby's friend and feeling so unliked and struggling with why he had to be like this. He sometimes felt like he was in the wrong body. He wondered if Ruby would still like him tomorrow. Just as he was about to turn his light out, his mom came in. Even though it was not talked about at the cookout, she knew something was going on. She had a feeling it had to do with Andrea.

"Are you ok Hector?" she asked. He started to cry,

"Why am I like this mom? Ruby's friend did not like me at all, she never even gave me a chance. I would have liked her," he whined.

Aww, Hector's mom felt like her heart was breaking. Why did other kids treat him like this? He has the sweetest heart and is so gentle, what's not to like? What could she say to him that would comfort him?

"Hector, you are the kindest, nicest boy I know, if others can't see that then there's something wrong with them. Don't ever try to change to be what someone else thinks you should be. Always have your own mind and respond with love no matter what. Your dad and I love you so much."

She put her arms around him and just loved him up until he stopped crying and started yawning. She tucked him in and turned out his light. Hector might have been tired but he did not sleep well that night. His mind, like Ruby's, would not stop thinking and racing. When he slept, he too dreamt. He dreamt that he had no one. No one at all and it was so lonely.

The next day Hector and Ruby stayed at home and moped around most of the day. They just couldn't understand why things had to be so hard. Hector's mom and Ruby's mom talked on the phone about how they could make them feel better, but they both knew that their kids had to work this out in their own way. Mom's cannot take away their children's pain no matter how hard they try, but it hurts them to watch them hurt and struggle.

Chapter Nine

The next day both moms decided it was time to get the two mopers out of the house. Ruby's dad had bought her a trampoline and it sat out there in the yard yet to be jumped on. Imagine that! When Ruby came down for breakfast, her mom suggested she invite Hector over to jump on the trampoline. Ruby really didn't seem to have an interest, but her mom insisted, so Ruby called Hector and invited him over. Hector came over with his head hanging low. He was still so sad. He and Ruby decided to take a little hike before jumping on the trampoline. As they walked along the path, they didn't seem to notice all the beauty around them like they usually did. Both of them knew they needed to talk about what happened, but both were unsure of how to start. It was awkward but Ruby started out with an apology.

"I'm sorry Hector," she said.

"What for? You didn't do anything," Hector replied.

Ruby told him she was sorry for how her friend acted towards him and how she felt like she was in the middle because she liked them both. Secretly Hector couldn't imagine what she liked about Andrea; she was just so nasty, not like Ruby at all.

"It's ok if you don't want to be my friend anymore, Ruby, I'm used to it. Pretty soon we'll be going back to school and I'm sure you have a lot of friends there too, they won't like me either, and I don't know why you did." Hector said.

Ruby was choked up; she didn't want to cry in front of Hector.

"Hector, I want to be your friend even when we go back to school, having lots of friends is a good thing. I like being your friend because you are nice and fun and funny too. Let's go back to my house now and jump on the trampoline!"

They headed back to Ruby's to jump and bounce. Ruby thought everything was all good now, but Hector was still feeling like this friendship was not going to last.

Wow! Ruby and Hector had so much fun jumping on the trampoline! It was in her yard for 2 weeks and she never went on it till today. Now she didn't want to get off! This was just what they both needed, a little exercise to help with the stress and tension they have been feeling. Ruby's mom even brought them out a picnic lunch to eat right on the trampoline. After they tired out, they went to Ruby's computer to look at YouTube videos of tricks they could learn to do on the trampoline. Before they knew it, Hector's mom was calling for him to come home for some dinner and family game night.

Ruby and her parents had a movie night complete with popcorn and lemonade. She was feeling better about Hector but still wondering about Andrea. Was she still going to be her friend? She wondered if she should call her, and after thinking about it, she decided to call her the next day.

Chapter Ten

When Ruby woke up the next morning, she was still tired. Her mind and dreaming kept her up again. She had so many feelings going on inside her. She was thinking about going on her trampoline and trying out some of those tricks her and Hector watched on YouTube, and she was excited about that. She also felt fear and dread over calling Andrea because she didn't know how Andrea was going to respond or what she was going to say to her. She didn't want to lose her as her friend, but then again, she didn't want to lose Hector either, even if he was a boy! So, she got up, made her bed and got dressed. Her hair could wait till later, or maybe her mom would help her with it today. After carefully arranging her stuffed animals on her bed, she went down stairs where her mom was making French Toast for breakfast.... yummy!

Ruby's mom put a plateful of French Toast on the table and poured the orange juice. As they ate together, Ruby brought up the subject of Andrea. Her mom thought it was a good idea to give Andrea a call and they thought and talked about what she would say to her. Ruby was still nervous about the call but knew she wanted to do it, so after breakfast she took the phone into her room to make the call.

"Hi! Can I talk to Andrea please?" Ruby said into the phone.

Andrea's mom hesitated. She was unsure if Andrea would come to the phone if she knew it was Ruby.

"Hold on, I'll see if she can come to the phone, Ruby," she said.

Ruby was chewing her lip waiting. She was so nervous.

"Hello?" Andrea said.

"Hi Andrea, this is Ruby,"

"I know," said Andrea, "what do you want?"

Oh boy thought Ruby, maybe *I shouldn't have called*. Ruby told her that she was sorry she left so early from the cookout and that she was sorry that she didn't like Hector, but hoped she would change her mind because she thought they were good friends and didn't want to give that up.

"Why do you like that loser and his dog so much?" Andrea asked.

Ruby was shocked; this wasn't going like she thought it would.

"Is he your REAL boyfriend or WHAT?" Andrea sarcastically asked.

Ruby didn't know what to say, obviously Andrea was still real mad and it didn't look like she was going to change her mind, so she apologized and told Andrea that she had to go. After she hung up, she just sat there on her bed still shocked. She thought for sure Andrea would come to her senses and see that they could all be friends, but I guess not. Ruby started to cry again. It felt like all she's done is cry for the last few days. She slowly walked back out to the kitchen where her mom was doing the dishes and cleaning up the kitchen. *Oh no*, her mom thought, *it doesn't look like it went well.* She went over to Ruby and put an arm around her and asked her what Andrea had to say. How could Ruby's mom help her to feel better? Sometimes it was hard to be the mom. She sure didn't have all the answers. So, she just kept hugging her and telling her that it would be ok. Maybe Andrea needed more time to think about it, it has only been a few days, but somehow Ruby's mom didn't think a few days would help this situation. It looked like Ruby was losing a friend because she stood up for a new friend who didn't look like others thought he should. Maybe Andrea was a little jealous too, afraid of losing Ruby's friendship. You just never know, but standing by what you think is right is always the right thing to do, even if it feels confusing and hurtful. Always be true to yourself.

Ruby asked her mom, "How do I have a good day when this has happened? How do I be?"

"Well," said Ruby's mom, "you can either mope in your room all day and keep thinking about it and doubting your decision, or you can try to put it aside in your mind and go about having a good day. It's a choice you can make. Every time it comes back in your mind, tell yourself that everything will work out. If you worry about it all day and spend the day in your room over it, it definitely won't fix it; it will just make you lose the opportunity to have a good day, and it won't make Andrea change her mind. You've done your part, now it's up to Andrea."

Ruby decided to take her mom's advice and call Hector to see what he was up to today, but he wasn't home. He and his mom went school clothes shopping, so Ruby thought she would try some of those new tricks on the trampoline by herself. She wanted to try the flip but she was scared! She went out to the trampoline, took her shoes off and started to jump, higher and higher she went, it was so fun! She loved how her pigtails flopped in the wind. She started out with the jump and then sit and then stand and once she gained confidence in that, she went right into a flip! *Wait till Hector see's this!* she thought. She couldn't wait till he got home to show him! So, she practiced for a little while until her mind started to bother her again. She kept thinking about Andrea and wishing she could be here to jump with her. She couldn't believe she was going to have to pick between her and Hector, it wasn't fair! She decided to go inside for a while and play with her stuffed animals.

Chapter Eleven

Hector begged his mom to take him to the Mall instead of Walmart for some "cooler" clothes. Hector was used to wearing hand me downs from friends; his dad had a new job and maybe now he could get some new clothes bought just for him. He had lost a little weight this summer from all the hiking, riding and jumping with Ruby. He hoped to keep that weight off and even lose more before school started, one less thing he could be made fun of for. So, they went to the Mall and went into stores like The Gap and Abercrombie, but Hector wasn't sure what was qualified as "cool" clothes. Maybe it didn't matter as long as they were bought at those stores and had a label on the outside to show where they were bought.

As they were coming out of The Gap with a few bags of new clothes they almost bumped into Andrea and her mom. *Oh no!* thought Hector! He thought for sure she would say something mean to him, but she just stuck her nose up in the air and walked right past him. He wasn't sure if that hurt his feelings more than if she would have insulted him, so he tried to just pretend it didn't happen. He didn't want to ruin his shopping trip; they still had Abercrombie to go to for some jeans and maybe a few new shirts. On the way home from the Mall, Hector's mom was driving down the Boulevard when a car went through a red light and smashed right into their car!

Hector flew forward when the air bag inflated to keep him from hitting the windshield. Hector's mom also flew forward but her air bag did not inflate so she hit against the steering wheel and hit her forehead on it. She was knocked out and Hector was frantic, he thought she was dead because there was blood on her face. People started to gather around the car to see if they were alright. He felt like a fish in a fish bowl with everyone looking in at them. Hector was so upset about his mom so when she started to move around and call Hector's name, he felt some relief. The driver of the other car came to the window to see if they were ok and someone called 911. Soon Hector could hear the sirens and became afraid again. When the paramedics came to the car to help them and check them both out, the people had to back up to let them by. The paramedics helped them out of the car and put his mom in the ambulance. Hector was allowed to ride along to the hospital.

His mom kept insisting that she was ok, but she had a cut on her head that would probably need some stitches. As they were pulling away from the scene of the accident Hector could see a tow truck loading up his moms crashed up car.

Hector took his mom's cell phone and called his dad to let him know what was happening. By the time they got to the hospital, Hector's dad was there too. He was so glad to see him.

"The car is ruined dad! The car is ruined!" Hector cried out to his dad.

His dad reassured him that they could get a new car, he was just glad they were both going to be ok. When they wheeled his mom out in a wheelchair with the bandage on her head, Hector thought he would faint. His dad had to hold him up; while his mom assured him, it looked worse than it was. On the way home, Hector was worried about so many things at once. He was worried about his mom, worried about the car and after a while, he worried about his purchases from the Mall! At least he had forgotten all about Andrea.

Ruby wondered how long Hector and his mom would be shopping; they had been gone a long time already. She knew because she was watching for the car to pull in the drive-way. His dad's car was there, but not his mom's. Did she miss it? After a while she called over there to see if maybe the car was in the garage. When Hector heard her voice, he just started to talk like she usually did…. all run on fast sentences as he told her about the accident… without stuttering.

"OMG," Ruby said.

She didn't know what else to say. She wanted to make sure they were both ok, but she didn't know what to say after that. After they calmed down after him telling her all the details, he started to tell her about the Mall. He wasn't sure if he wanted to tell her about Andrea, so he skipped that part. But now his new clothes were in the car and the car was towed somewhere, so he didn't know when he would get them back. Hector asked her to hold on a minute and went to ask his parents if Ruby could come over and play video games with him for a little while. With permission he then asked Ruby to come over.

Ruby wasn't sure what Hector's mom would look like since she never seen stitches before. She imagined his mom would have a big bloody bandage on her head and she was a little nervous about that. But when she got there and seen it was just a little bandage and his mom was acting all normal, she relaxed a bit. Her and

Hector started out with Pac Man and Hector also brought out some of his stuffed animals. Ruby was impressed.

Chapter Twelve

The next morning Hector really wanted to go into the woods and explore. Summer was getting shorter and soon he would be getting ready to go to his new school. Middle school…. he was not looking forward to being the new kid in class. Before calling Ruby to see if she wanted to go to the woods, he wanted to make sure his mom was going to be ok today. Maybe he needed to stay home and take care of her. As he headed downstairs for breakfast, he could smell the bacon cooking…. mmmm, nothing like the smell of bacon! His mom was cooking scrambled eggs and bacon and she looked like she was ok, but he asked her anyways.

"Just a little headache," she said, "I think I'll take it easy today."

"Good idea," Hector said. "Do you want me to stay home and take care of you?"

"No, no, no…you go have fun with Ruby, I'll be ok," his mom reassured him.

Ruby was good with going to the woods, so she got dressed and wore her rain boots just in case they wanted to get closer to the edge of the pond. They met in the middle of their yards and together with Ranger they headed for the woods, both in rain boots and each carrying a bucket for treasures. It was so much cooler in the woods. They stopped at the tire swing and took turns swinging for a while before taking the path further into the woods. Hector decided to fill his bucket with wild flowers for his mom and Ruby decided to do the same. There were flowers of all colors, so pretty! His mom would be so surprised, Hector thought. And the bouquet would be HUGE!

As they were walking along, they both heard a tiny animal sound, *probably a bird*, they both thought. Suddenly they came upon it and it was a bird, a baby bird. Ranger started to bark. It must have fallen out of the nest they saw up in the tree. They both crouched down in awe to take a peek at the tiny bird. Ranger was quiet then, just watching with his tail wagging.

"I think it's crying for its mom," Ruby said.

"I think so too," said Hector.

They stayed there crouched down just watching the little bird for a while before they decided they needed to do something about it. They agreed to put all the flowers in one bucket and take the little bird home with them. Both were sure their parents would know what to do. They pulled some grass and put it in the bucket first before Hector gently picked up the baby bird and laid it in the grass inside the bucket.

"He looks hungry," Said Ruby.

Well birds eat worms so they looked around to see if they could find some worms to take home with them. Ranger laid down under the tree as if watching to see what would happen next. Suddenly the mother bird swooped down at them hitting Ruby in the head. She was holding the bucket with the baby bird in it and almost dropped it. Ruby screamed and the baby bird screeched as if it were saying, "I'm in here mom!" The bird kept swooping down at them screeching all the time.

"What should we do Hector?" yelled Ruby.

They couldn't reach to put the bird back up in the tree, but it was clear that the mom bird wanted her baby back. They decided to put the bird back on the ground where they found it and hide to see if the mom would take care of it. Hector attempted to set it back in the grass even while the mom bird continued to swoop with that screeching sound. WAM! It hit him in the head one more time before he put it safely in the grass. They hid behind a nearby tree and waited to see what would happen. Thankfully Ranger followed them. He was probably afraid of the mom bird! Finally, the mom bird stopped screeching and swooped down to her baby. She kept hopping around it as if to protect it. The tiny bird kept screeching until the mom bird sat on it.

"Maybe it's cold," Ruby whispered.

After a few minutes the mom bird started to go a little distance from the baby bird, gathering small sticks and putting them around the baby. She was hiding it! So maybe she would take care of it. Ruby and Hector continued to watch, fascinated at the work the mom bird was doing. When she had the baby surrounded with sticks and grass, she flew off and, in a few minutes, she was back with a worm hanging from her beak. She was going to feed her baby. Both Hector and Ruby realized that they would not be taking the baby bird home. They quietly got up and moved away from the mom and her baby. Ranger wanted to stay, so Hector had to take him by the collar to get him moving. They decided they would stop on their way back to see if everything was going well for the mom bird and her baby.

Chapter Thirteen

Ruby and Hector explored a little further, picked a few more flowers and then headed back to see if the baby bird was doing ok and the mom bird was taking care of it. Ruby, Hector, and Ranger quietly crept up to the tree near where the baby bird was. They could see the mom bird sitting on top of the grass and sticks she put over the baby. She was still taking care of it, but they wondered if there were more babies in the nest. There was no way they could climb up the tree to check it out and even if they could it probably was not a good idea. So, they crept away as quietly as they had come and headed for home.

Ruby and Hector couldn't wait to tell their parents what happened in the woods. First, they went to Hector's so they could check on his mom and give her the flowers they picked for her. She was lying on the couch watching Law and Order. She seemed to be ok and was so surprised with the flowers. She loved them. And the story they had to tell! She laughed and was serious too. They did the right thing she said. Nature has a way of taking care of itself. But she probably would have brought the baby bird home too if the mom was not going to take care of it. Hector and Ruby decided to go back the next day to check on it.

Next, they went to Ruby's house to tell her mom about it. Ruby, of course, was talking really fast and running her words together so Hector had to jump in there a few times to give her mom the slower version. Ruby's mom said much of the same thing that Hector's mom did. She told them she was proud of them for letting the mom bird take over. She thought it was a little funny how the bird rammed them in the head when they had the baby in the bucket.

Ruby's mom made them peanut butter and jelly sandwiches and milkshakes for lunch before they went out to jump on the trampoline for a while. Ruby showed Hector some of her new moves and he was impressed and eager to learn. She showed him the jump, sit, and stand and he caught on really quick. Ranger was running around the trampoline all excited about all the laughing and jumping.

While Ruby and Hector were playing on the trampoline, her mom made a meal for Hector's family so that his mom could rest. She made her a tuna noodle casserole. When Hector went home, she and Ruby walked with him to take the dinner in person and to see how his mom was doing. "What a beautiful bouquet!" Ruby's mom said when she saw the flowers in a vase. Hector's mom smiled big, she loved them too. Ruby and Hector stood a little taller with pride in their gift. Ruby stayed a little while and her mom asked if there was anything she could do before she left, but Hectors mom was ok so she headed home to make a dinner for her family. Ruby hoped for home fries and hot dogs, but her mom already made a casserole for them too. When they got home her dad called to make sure she was going to be there, he had a surprise for Ruby!

Oh boy! Ruby was excited! What could the surprise be? Ruby could hardly wait. What could she do till her dad got home in an hour? Her mom told her to go out and jump for a little while to help with her excitement. As Ruby jumped, she tried to imagine the surprise. This was the first she heard of it and it didn't seem like her mom knew, so maybe it was a surprise for both of them. Maybe a trip to Disney! Maybe a new bike! Whatever it was, she would have to wait.

Chapter Fourteen

Ruby was laying on her belly watching TV when she heard her dad's car in the drive-way. She jumped up and went racing to the door when her mom stopped her. She told her to go back in the living room and sit on the couch to wait till her dad came in the house. Ruby slunk back to the couch, she didn't want to wait any longer! Well in he came, carrying a box. *Hmmm, what could be in the box??* thought Ruby.

"What is it dad? What is it?" Ruby exclaimed excitedly.

"Calm down Ruby," her mom said, "you'll scare it."

Ok, so now it wasn't a trip to Disney, or a new bike but something alive! Her dad set the box down in front of her and told her to go ahead and open it. She was sooooo excited! When she opened the box there was a tiny white ball of fur jumping to get out of the box! Ruby picked it up and hugged it while squealing with delight.

"A dog! It's my very own dog!" Ruby squealed.

The little dog was licking her face and squirming like crazy! "What will you name her

Ruby?" said her mom. Ruby thought about it for a moment and then said, "I'm going to name her, Bonnet! Bonnet will be her name!"

Ruby set Bonnet down on the floor and watched her run around. Her dad went back to the car to get the dog supplies. Ruby couldn't believe she had her own dog! She wondered how Ranger would like her and Hector too. Hector! She had to call him! "Mom, mom, can I call Hector and tell him and Ranger to come over?" Ruby called out to her mom who went into the kitchen to help her dad with the supplies. "Maybe you should wait a little while and let Bonnet get used to you before you invite him and Ranger over," said her mom. "Ok," said Ruby, she wasn't disappointed because she had a handful of a puppy that wanted her attention! Later was good.

There were so many supplies for such a little dog! There was a leash, some food bowls, and toys, treats, and a crate with a soft red cushion with paw prints on it. Her collar was red with sparkles on it! *Dad thought of everything!* Ruby thought with love. She grabbed onto some of the toys and started to play with Bonnet. Boy, Bonnet sure had a lot of energy! She raced around the room a few times and then came to Ruby for a toy. They were having so much fun, until Bonnet decided to pee on the floor! "OH NO!" exclaimed Ruby's mom. Her dad scooped her up and took her outside, but it was too late. So, they decided that in a little while they would take her out and see if she would go and then give her treats if she did. Ruby's mom cleaned up the mess with a little frown on her face. *What did we get ourselves into here?* she thought. But Ruby was just so excited to have her very own dog!

A little while later, her dad asked her if she wanted to take Bonnet for a walk. They could introduce Bonnet to Ranger and Hector. Ruby made a dash for her shoes and the leash. Bonnet was never on a leash before so she wasn't a real good walker, she mostly tried to run and it looked like she'd choke to death before they got to Hector's, so Ruby picked her up. I guess some dog training would be how she spent the rest of her vacation! Hector was so surprised when he opened the door and seen the little puppy in Ruby's arms. Ranger came running out, barking all the way. Ruby was a little afraid to put Bonnet down, she didn't know what Ranger would do, but then she remembered how gentle he was with the baby bird, so she leaned over and set Bonnet on the ground. Ranger was all over her, sniffing everywhere, and it looked like Bonnet was liking every minute of it. She was doing her fair share of sniffing too! Looks like Ranger found a friend this summer too!

When they got home, Ruby's dad had a list of responsibilities that Ruby would have as a new dog owner. The list seemed pretty long, but Ruby didn't care, she had her very own dog!! Bonnet!! She would have to let her out to go to the bathroom and walk her. She could sleep in Ruby's room, but she had to go in her crate because they really couldn't trust her yet to roam the house. First things first.... potty training. Ruby would also be the pooper scooper in the yard. Now that was a big responsibility! After Bonnet calmed down a little bit, Ruby went to her computer and googled How to Train a Puppy.

The first rule was to let your puppy know who was in charge and to teach her to come when you call her and to reward her when she listened. Ruby felt like they were going to need a lot of treats. This puppy training looked a little overwhelming!

"Time for dinner," Ruby's mom called. Ruby was definitely not hungry, but she knew she had to sit for dinner.

"What will Bonnet do while we eat dinner?" Ruby asked.

"We'll just let her explore the house while we eat and then after dinner you can take her outside so she doesn't pee in the house again, now go wash your hands," said her dad.

During dinner Bonnet kept coming to Ruby's chair whining for food off her plate. "Do not give her anything from the table Ruby," her mom said, "She'll expect it all the time and we don't want that habit." Bonnet had to go to her crate for the first time where she cried and fussed all though dinner. Ruby felt bad for her and tried to hurry her dinner along.

After dinner Ruby had to help clear the table before letting Bonnet out of her crate. She hurried! Since the yard is fenced in, she didn't have to put Bonnet on a leash. What a good girl she was, she pooped and peed outside so when they got back inside, she got two treats. Ruby spent the rest of the evening teaching her to come when she called her. She was going to like being a dog owner! She wished she could have Andrea over to meet Bonnet, but she knew that wasn't going to happen.

Chapter Fifteen

The next day Ruby and Hector played in the yard all day with Bonnet and Ranger. Hector was showing her some tricks Ranger could do and Ruby was anxious to teach Bonnet everything. They couldn't take Bonnet to the woods yet; she was too young and didn't obey well enough yet. So, they were content to stay put in the yard, jumping and playing with their dogs. Hector showed Ruby how Ranger could play catch with the Frisbee and Ruby thought that was so cool, but Bonnet would have to learn how to fetch before she advanced to playing catch. She would just chew up the Frisbee! When Ruby threw a ball or a toy to her, she would go get it, but she would keep it to chew on for a while. Bonnet had a lot to learn and so did Ruby!

Ruby was warm so she kicked off her shoes and her and Hector decided to try and play with the Frisbee without Ranger. It was a challenge because Ranger thought it was just for him. Hector threw it to Ruby and she ran to get it before Ranger. Just as she was about to catch it, she screamed out in pain and dropped to the ground. Hector came running to see what was wrong. Her foot! It hurt so badly! It was stinging and hurting and she felt like she was going to cry. She sat on the grass and Bonnet and Ranger thought she was sitting down to play with them so they came running to her, but she was in no mood to play so she shooed them away, Hector helped with that. Ruby looked at the bottom of her foot and saw a red blotch starting to swell, and boy did it hurt! Hector went inside to get Ruby's mom and she knew right away it was a bee sting, so she examined it to see if the stinger was still inside and it was. Ruby was holding her foot like someone was going to steal it while her mom went inside to get some tweezers. Ruby was afraid it was going to hurt worse to have her mom take the stinger out. Her mom brought an ice cube out with her and put it right on the sting. To Ruby's surprise, the ice took some of the pain away, but she was still afraid to let her mom use the tweezers on her. Her mom comforted her and reassured her that it would feel much better after she got that little black stinger out, so Ruby let her do it while she scrunched her eyes shut to keep in the tears of fear inside.

One pluck and it was out and it did feel a little better and not too painful coming out. Her mom helped her up and she sat on one of the lawn chairs with her foot on a stool. Hector was hovering around wondering what he should do. Ruby's mom suggested they relax, have a treat and maybe play some board games till she felt better. She went inside to get them a selection of games to choose from.

They chose Monopoly and Ruby set it up while Hector made sure the dogs had water to drink. Ruby's mom brought out some strawberries and whipped cream…. oh yum!

After the game, which takes a long time to play, Ruby felt like she could put her socks and shoes back on and get back to dog training and playing. She couldn't believe how much better it felt because it looked and felt like it would hurt forever when it first happened, now she could barely see where it was. They have a lot of dandelions in their yard, and she loves them, but so do the bees!

That afternoon went by really quick. They had the weekend, and then back to school on Monday. The summer went by so quick. Ruby still had not heard from Andrea and she was sad to lose a good friend, but what if another new friend came into Ruby's life, would Andrea not like them either? Did she want to have only one friend? Ruby liked to have lots of friends, all different kinds of friends. Someday Andrea might change her mind.

After dinner, Ruby and her mom were going school clothes shopping. Ruby was excited to get some new clothes, a new backpack and some new sneakers. Her dad was also going out, he bowled on Friday nights, and so Bonnet would have to be in her crate for a few hours while they were gone. She still didn't like her crate, but they still could not trust her to leave her roam the house.

They went to the mall and Ruby picked out some cute new clothes, cool too! After they had all the shopping done, they decided to get ice cream. Ruby's favorite! *hmmm, root beer float, hot fudge sundae, or a banana split?* thought Ruby. Ruby decided to go with the banana split, it was big but she thought she could do it and she did. Her mom got a hot fudge sundae. While they were eating their ice cream, they talked about going into middle school. Ruby was a little nervous about it. It was a big school with older kids there too. Kids that looked older than the older kids when she was in elementary school. And there was changing classes. She was afraid she would get lost and be late and get in trouble. Her mom told her that they would all be new to the school and so getting lost and being late the first few days was probably ok. After the first week she would know where she was going and she would probably end up liking the moving around during the day and having different teachers.

"And what about Hector? What if the other kids didn't like him either? What about Andrea? Should I try to talk to her?" Ruby rattled on with all her worries. Her ice cream was starting to melt! Her mom tried to calm her fears, but it's normal to have fears when going somewhere new. Growing up was not easy! She was going to be a teenager this year! Ruby loved her mom so much; she always had good answers for Ruby's problems.

Chapter Sixteen

Hector and Ruby were both excited and nervous about starting school on Monday. The bus stop was right out front and they would ride together. Both could not wait to wear their new clothes but Hector was really nervous. In his previous school he got bullied so much. Kids never gave him a chance because of the way he looked and he didn't think he was very smart either. He never raised his hand even though he knew the answer and when they had to work in teams, nobody wanted him on their team. It was embarrassing and humiliating and he would start sweating when he was the only one left without a partner. The teacher would then assign him to a team and they would all snicker and giggle when he would be forced to join them. Hector was a little over weight and his clothes had always been hand me downs from his mom's friends' kids. Some fit good and others just didn't look that great. He knew it, but he felt it didn't matter, kids made fun of him whatever he wore. Hector was kind of hopeless in school. His parents just didn't have a lot of money to buy nice clothes but he never complained. He hoped that in this new school with his new clothes it was be better this year, and he had one friend already. But he still had his doubts about Ruby going off with all her friends that she already had...like Andrea. He hoped to get a few friends of his own, maybe some boys.

Kids in his old school used to say things like, Fatty fatty two by four couldn't fit through the bathroom door, fatso, tubby, dummy, and stupid... all nasty names and they were not quiet about it either. Sometimes when the teacher wasn't looking someone would shove him or knock his books off his desk. Hector often cried inside his mind during school, just wanting to go home. The bus ride home was even worse, no one wanted to sit with him and the name calling would be worse than it was during school. The bigger boys would threaten to beat him up. His heart ached too, and he always wondered what was wrong with him. Well no one gave him a chance. And no one ever spoke up for him either, they were afraid if they did, they would then get made fun of too. But what about the teachers and the bus aid, did they hate him too? Being in 6th grade this year meant changing for gym class, and swimming. Hector was definitely not looking forward to taking his clothes off in front of everyone, then they would really see his body. His dread was bigger than his excitement. This summer had been the best ever and he didn't want it to end. For once he had a friend that didn't seem to mind his appearance or how he stuttered sometimes and that was about to end for him. How embarrassing it was going to be when it all started and Ruby would see how everyone hated him.

So now it was Sunday, the last day of summer vacation. Hector hoped it wasn't the last day of having a friend. What would they do for their last day? He wanted it to be special and fun. Both sets of parents thought it would be fun to go to the amusement park together for the last day of summer vacation and Ruby and Hector were all for it! Both families packed up a lunch and some sun screen and off they went. Bonnet, of course, had to stay back in her crate for the day, but Ruby promised her a walk in the woods when she came home.

Chapter Seventeen

Ruby rode in Hectors car on the way to the park. They talked about what rides they wanted to go on and which ones they were afraid of. Ruby talked about the splash park but Hector told her he didn't bring his suit. He didn't tell her it was because he was ashamed of his body. "What's your favorite ride Hector, Ruby asked. "Hmmm," Hector thought for a few minutes, "I think my favorite ride is the Pirate Ride...it's so fun, let's go on that lots of times!" Ruby liked the roller coasters, her favorite one was called The Sky Coaster. It was really high up and the ride down was so scary, but so fun! They decided to go on all the rides at least once, even the scariest looking ones.

When they got to the park, it looked like everyone had the same idea. There were so many people there already and they got there early. The ride lines would be long. They found a parking space, but it was pretty far from the entrance, oh well, a little more exercise for the day! Everyone carried something. Once they got inside the park with all the coolers and supplies for the day, they had to find a picnic table that wasn't already taken. The one they found was right smack in the middle of everyone else. When everything was unpacked and sun screen put on, they headed to the rides. Ruby and Hector were excited! They decided to start out with the non-scary rides first, so they ran to get in line at the Bumper Cars and then the Ferris Wheel. The parents just followed along behind while Ruby and Hector ran from ride to ride.

They rode the rides all morning before going back to the picnic area for lunch. Ruby's mom and dad brought the hot dogs so her dad was getting the fire going in the grill. Out came the macaroni salads and chips and drinks. Ruby and Hector were hungry from running all morning, but were anxious to get back to the rides.

"You need to power up your body to keep going," Ruby's dad said.

"Ok, Ok," said both Ruby and Hector at the same time. They all laughed.

After lunch the parents decided to give Ruby and Hector some time to run by themselves. Since they were 12, they would have to start learning to do things on their own without their parent's right there. The parents would stay at the picnic area and play cards for a while. "Stay together and don't forget not to talk to strangers," said Hector's dad. "Be back here in two hours". They both had watches on, so Hector and Ruby set out for the rides. They were happy to be on their own. They went on the roller coasters two times each and decided to go on the Ferris Wheel for a slowdown ride before going on the Tilt a Whirl. Hector had to use the bathroom first so Ruby told him she's wait near the Tilt-a-Whirl. After all they couldn't stay together in the bathrooms!

When Hector came out of the bathroom, Ruby was not where she said she'd be and he felt a little panicked, but not real scared yet. He walked around the ride and tried to look at the riders on the ride but it was going so fast they were blurred. He waited in the spot she said she'd be figuring she'd be back but after about 15 minutes he began to get scared. He wasn't sure if he should go back to the picnic area or look for her. After another 5 minutes he decided to go back to the picnic area and see if she was there. He was so scared!

Ruby was lost. She had waited in the spot she told Hector she would be for a few minutes, but thought she would just explore a little bit before he got back and now, she couldn't find her way back. She looked around and couldn't see the

Tilt-a-Whirl anymore. She got scared and didn't know what to do. She kept walking hoping that something would look familiar, but that wasn't happening. *Oh, why did I wander*, she thought. She was fighting to not cry. Everyone looked like a stranger. She was scared!

Hector thought he was headed to the picnic area but soon realized that he went the wrong way. Now he was lost. Which way had he come from? *Oh no*, he thought, *what am I going to do now?* He looked around and tried to figure out the right way back to the Tilt-a-Whirl but it all looked the same. Everyone looked like a stranger. He was scared!

Hector's dad looked at his watch for the 10th time. It was getting close to two hours since the kids were gone on their own. They should be coming back any minute now. The moms were cleaning up the picnic area, getting ready to leave. They didn't seem worried. They knew the kids would stay together and be back on time, they were responsible kids. Well after about 15 more minutes, they all started to get worried. The dad's decided to go out looking for them. They had their cell phones with them to call and let each other know if they found them. Ruby's mom hoped they just lost track of time and would be coming along soon.

Ruby somehow found her way back to the Tilt-a-Whirl but Hector was nowhere to be found. She thought she should go back to the picnic area and let the parents know that Hector was lost, but now she forgot which way to go. The park was so big. She might have found the Tilt-a-Whirl but she was lost too. Tears started to fall from her eyes. The ride attendant noticed her standing there crying so he approached her to see if he could help. *Is this a stranger?* she thought. Should she ask him for help? He didn't know who Hector was. She walked away quickly before he got to her. Suddenly she saw a police officer. *That's no stranger...* she thought, *that's a police man, they help people, right?* Oh wait, the police officer was a police woman.

Should she go to her and ask for help? {{{{YES!! Go to her Ruby!}}}} Ruby was nervous. She knew she needed help. The officer noticed her and started to walk towards her. Ruby waited. She was crying now.

"Do you need some help? Are you lost little girl?" the police woman said. Ruby just shook her head.

"Well you just come with me, we'll find your parents...try not to worry," said the police woman. "They are probably looking for you too," she said. Ruby walked alongside the police woman and felt a little bit better, but was still scared for Hector, where could he be? They walked to a little station set up for the police and had her sit down. She got her some water and Kleenex and let her just sit for a moment till she calmed down a little bit.

"Ok, so tell me your name and your parent's name, are they here with you today?"

"Oh yes," Ruby said, she was trying to talk slowly enough that her words did not blur together like they usually did. She told the police woman her whole story about her parent's telling them to stay together and Hector going to the bathroom and her wandering away to explore. "Hector is lost," Ruby cried, "you have to find him!"

"Ok, Ok, let's just be calm and we will find Hector too." She went to her radio and talked into it giving Hector's description and age to the other police officers out there walking around. It was almost 1 hour since they were supposed to be back at the picnic area, her parents would be worried!

Suddenly the door opened and in came Hector with another officer. Ruby never felt so relieved in her life! She was so glad to see him, she ran to him to hug him and tell him she was sorry for wandering. Hector looked relieved too. Now they just had to find their parents! But not to worry, soon after that, both dads came through the door and boy were they happy to see their kids! Ruby's dad took out his phone right away and called her mom to let them know they found them. Then Ruby thought they might be mad at them but that could wait till later...they were just happy to see them and that they were ok.

On the way home, Ruby rode with her parents and Hector rode with his parents. They both had a story to tell and both sets of parents wanted to hear it. It started out to be a great day but getting lost sure can suck the fun out of the day! Ruby and Hector were tired out and couldn't wait to get home.

Chapter Eighteen

Ruby and Hector were so glad to be home! Ruby went right to Bonnet's crate and let her out. She was glad Ruby was home too! Ruby took her out back to go to the bathroom right away. Her mom and dad talked to her about getting lost at the park today and told her that she did the right thing in trusting the police officer, but next time DON'T WANDER! They weren't mad at her but were firm about the: don't wander! A similar conversation went on at Hector's house.

Ok, so this was the last night of summer vacation. Ruby wanted to be all ready for school tomorrow. She was still nervous about middle school, but excited too. She wanted to look just right. Ruby set out her outfit and her new sneakers and back pack. She couldn't wait to get her list of supplies, she loved picking out new folders and pencils. Bonnet was running around her room chewing on Ruby's old sneaker. She took it away from her and gave her one of her dog toys instead. Her old sneakers would be good for walking in the woods, but not with holes in them!

"Off to bed early tonight," her mom said.

"I know, I know…and I'm tired out anyways!" Ruby answered. Her mom helped her to brush out her hair after her shower. Ruby wanted to paint her nails too…she was a 6th grader now you know. Her mom would braid her hair in the morning.

Hector was in his room deciding what outfit to wear for the first day of school. He was so nervous and maybe a little hopeful too. He had all new clothes and new sneakers too. He hoped kids would like him this year. His mom came in to remind him that he needed to get into bed a little earlier tonight. It would take a few days to get back in the habit of getting up early. She noticed he was a little nervous and so she asked him if everything was ok. Hector repeated his fears again. What could she do as a mom to make sure he had a good day at school? She felt helpless. She told him to be himself and not let anyone take away his goodness. She hoped he would make some new friends this year. It's been a little rough the past couple of years with kids bullying her son. She had been to the school and talked to the principal and the teachers but it seemed like nothing ever changed. They just bullied out of sight of the teachers. She hoped this new school year would be a better fit for him. He had such a nice summer and she hoped it would continue in school.

Ranger and Bonnet were lucky that Hector's mom and Ruby's mom were home during the day. Ranger could be let out a few times during the day and Bonnet didn't have to be in her crate all day, but they sure would miss the all day playing with Hector and Ruby.

Goodnight Hector......Good night Ruby

Sweet Dreams

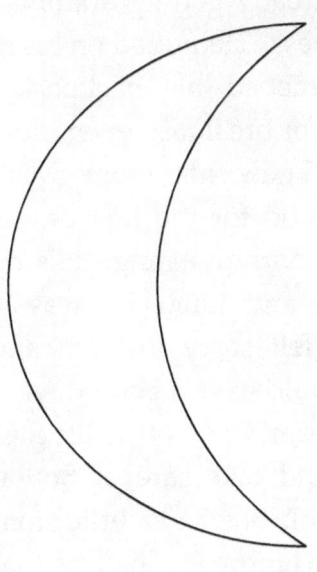

Chapter Nineteen

Buzzzzz, Hector's alarm clock went off, time to get up for school. He laid there and thought about it for a few minutes. His mom stuck her head in the door to make sure he was awake.

"I'm coming, I'm coming," said Hector. He rolled out of bed, Ranger right next to him, wagging his tail probably wondering what they were going to do today. "Sorry Ranger, it's back to school today," Hector told him with his head hanging low.

He was already getting a stomach ache from his nervousness. He pulled on his new jeans and tee shirt, grabbed his backpack and headed down stairs for breakfast, even though he wasn't hungry he knew his mom was cooking up something good for the first day of school and would insist on him eating. His mom took one look at him and knew he wasn't feeling too good. She felt sorry for him and once more hoped he would have a good day.

Ruby's alarm went off a little early to make sure she could take care of Bonnet before she went to school. She had a little stomach ache but was trying to ignore it. She was looking forward to seeing all her friends and new teachers, but still nervous about getting lost and about the whole Hector/Andrea situation. She could smell the bacon cooking downstairs and hurried Bonnet along out to the yard before she sat down for bacon and eggs. After breakfast she went back up to her room to get dressed and get her hair combed out so her mom could braid it for her.

"Mom, what should I do if other kids start bothering Hector like Andrea did?" asked Ruby.

"Well honey, all you can do is be his friend. Stand by him and show the others that you are his friend." Her mom replied.

"What if they start doing it to me?" she asked with fear.

"That's the chance you have to take Ruby, you can show that you've made the decision to pick the friends you want no matter what others think of them or you. It's probably not going to be easy, but your heart will feel better for it. And when your heart feels better, your mind has an easier time of accepting it too," her mom said with love. She was hoping it wouldn't come to this but Ruby really had to decide what kind of person she wanted to be. It is part of growing up.

At 9:00 AM Ruby and Hector met out front to wait for the bus. Both were glad to see each other, but both were also nervous. They both just shuffled their feet and didn't say much. *This is probably the last time Ruby will talk to me like a friend.* Hector thought sadly. But he could not think of one thing to say.

"I'm sure we won't be in the same homeroom, Hector, but maybe we will be able to have lunch together," Ruby said. *Sure,* Hector thought. *Wait till she sees what happens to me at school, or even on the bus.*

Here came the bus around the corner. Hector thought he was going to throw up, so he took some deep breaths and got ready to get on the bus. Hector got on first, remembering his bus rides from his other school where he would get tripped or his backpack taken and tossed around. There were only a few kids at the back of the bus and they didn't pay him much attention. Ruby got on next and the kids on the bus all called out HI's to her. She seemed happy to see them. Hector took a seat near the front and Ruby sat with him. Still neither one knew what to say to each other. Ruby wondered if she should introduce him to her friends. She turned around and started to introduce her new friend to her old friends. They all said hi, but that was it. He sat quietly. He tried to hold his head up but wondered if they were staring at him. The bus filled up along the way and everyone seemed to know Ruby. Hector was impressed, but still nervous. *Maybe having Ruby as a friend would help him to have friends and be popular*, he thought hopefully.

Chapter Twenty

They arrived at school and Ruby realized that her mom was right; no one really knew where they were going. They all got inside the school and just stood around wondering where to go first. There were older kids in the halls to show them the way. They wore name tags and started to ask what room they were looking for and taking groups at a time to their homeroom. Ruby wondered if they would be around all day to help them find their other class rooms. She hoped so!

This is where Ruby and Hector separated. They both just quietly followed their guide. Ruby was soon chatting and laughing with her friends and telling them about Bonnet. Others were talking about their summer vacation and where they went. They got into homeroom and met their teacher. She seemed nice, but also somehow different from her teachers in elementary school. Maybe they would be stricter in middle school, she didn't know. And maybe she would have more homework too, ugh. So far, she was doing good, she felt like she was relaxing a little bit, probably from being with her friends. There were a lot of kids she didn't know too.

The day started and Mrs. Mayberry stood before them telling them the rules of homeroom and told them she would help them find their next class and their lockers. Ruby hoped she could work the combination ok and remember it too.   It turned out that everyone traveled through the day with their homeroom class, so these would be the kids she would have in every class every day. She looked around to see everybody. Some were new kids and some were kids she went to elementary school with. All were talking to each other, which made it loud when Mrs. Mayberry let them know that they needed to be quiet and listen to what she had to say. She told them that when they arrived in the mornings, they could talk to each other until the bell rang, then it was time to take a seat for attendance, announcements, and the Pledge of Allegiance.

Hector arrived in his homeroom and found a seat. He looked around at all the new faces. One boy was talking loudly to others. They seemed to be listening intently to what he had to say. He was laughing and seemed a little over powering.

The boy sitting across from him started to talk to him… "What school are you coming from?" he asked.

Hmm, thought Hector, *maybe this will be a new friend!* He started to relax a little bit and quietly answered his questions. He never thought to ask the same questions back. He looked at this boy that talked to him to see what he looked like and what kind of clothes he was wearing, but it didn't really matter to Hector, this kid seemed nice! He talked to him and didn't make fun of him yet. Hector wondered if it was because of his new clothes, and decided it must be. He was still a little bit overweight, but he took more care on combing his hair. He thought his appearance helped him so far. His new look! Trying to look better on the outside.

When the bell rang his homeroom teacher, Mr. Fink told them to all line up and he would give them a little tour and show them their lockers. They each had their combinations in their backpack so they took them out to see what number locker they had. Mr. Fink made an example of Hectors locker combination. It looked pretty easy, but when Hector tried it, it didn't work. He started to panic, so Mr. Fink started over, showed him and then guided him through it and then moved on to others who were having trouble. Soon they all had it figured out. It turned out all of the classes would be pretty close by to the other ones. *This might turn out better than I thought*, thought Hector. He started to relax a little more as he stood to walk behind the others for the tour. The boy who talked to him, Rodney, walked behind Hector.

Rodney was scared, thinking about when the bullying would start. His stomach was just churning around in there, making all kinds of noises. He was afraid someone would hear them and start in on him about it. There were a few of his former classmates in his group. They hadn't bothered him yet. He wasn't sure if Hector liked him or not but at least he didn't ignore him or say something mean to him. Maybe they could be friends. As he walked along behind Hector suddenly a foot came out and before he could catch himself, he felt himself falling into Hector. And so it started. The laugh from the loud mouth boy was heard by the whole class and brought more attention to the trip. Some kids were laughing and some were extra quiet. The teacher didn't notice, he was already out the door. Rodney apologized to Hector for pushing against him. Hector wasn't sure how to respond. If he was nice to Rodney would the others start on him? Rodney seemed like he would be a good friend, but Hector was hoping to be in with the popular people this year. Hector didn't say anything to Rodney; he barely looked at him and kept walking. He didn't feel right about it, but hoped he was doing the right thing. Then Hector saw her…Andrea. They passed each other in the hall and she gave him such looks that it made him shrink inside himself in fear. He was more used to being bullied by boys, but Andrea, she looked so mean. He was glad she was not in his group. Rodney didn't try to talk to Hector again that day. Hector felt confused.

Hector felt like things were going ok, sort of, at least he didn't get shoved, pushed or made fun of yet. He could see that the boy he thought could be his friend was having a rough day. He felt sorry for him, but still didn't stand by him. Being popular was important to him this year and he didn't want to jeopardize it by hanging out with someone that was obviously not popular. But Hector couldn't figure it out; Rodney looked like a popular kid, why was he bullied?

Finally, it was lunch time! Hector looked around for Ruby. There she was! Sitting alone at a table unpacking her lunch, so Hector went over. On his way, he noticed Rodney sitting alone, but he walked right by him. Rodney looked so lonely, but Hector wanted to be with the popular kids so he went over and took a seat across from Ruby. He hoped all the kids in his group would see who he was sitting with. Soon Ruby's table filled up and everyone was chatting with each other about their first morning in middle school. Hector didn't say one word, and felt very out of place, but he didn't want to be any place else. No one was really giving him any attention. He wasn't sure if he liked that or not. Ruby was talking with everyone, he felt a little left out by her, maybe even jealous, but at the same time he felt so grateful to be sitting at the lunch table with all the cool kids, he really hoped that the kids in his group would see him. Andrea was at another table with more popular kids. Every once in a while, she looked over at him and gave him that look that made him worry about what she was going to do. He wondered if she and Ruby talked or if they were in the same homeroom. He'd ask Ruby later. Hector managed to eat all his lunch and then the bell rang. Time to go back to class. He walked right by Rodney and didn't even act like he saw him sitting alone.

Rodney was feeling very sad and lonely. What was it about him that nobody liked? If he knew that he might be able to change it. He wanted to cry, but he learned that boys don't cry, so he cried on the inside.

Chapter Twenty-One

Two more classes then the first day of school would be over. Hector felt like he was holding his breath. Not one incident of bullying happened to him today yet. Hopefully the bus ride home would be ok too. He felt good but he felt something nagging at him. He of all people should know how it feels to be bullied, and yet when someone else was on that end of things, he did nothing. He always wondered why no one helped him. What could he do though? It started to bother him more that he thought it should.

The last bell rang and everyone headed to their lockers. Ruby got her locker open on the first try. Her locker was not near Hector's locker. She got her backpack out and shut the door thinking about how she could decorate inside of the door, she knew she wanted a mirror for sure.

Hector was having a little trouble with his combination lock. It took him a few times and some frustration before he got it open. He took out his backpack and turned around to see if Ruby was coming for him, but she was nowhere in sight. He wondered if he should just head out to the bus or wait for her, they hadn't talked about it. Rodney was a few lockers away. He looked over at Hector hopefully, but Hector looked away.

Hector decided to go out to the bus. It was ok on the way there, so he felt almost confident it would be ok for the ride home too. He took a seat near the front. Always near the front because then he was near the bus driver and less likely to be bothered. The fights and bullying usually took place at the back of the bus. Rodney stepped onto the bus and looked over at Hector as if asking to sit with him. He sat looking out the window for Ruby, paying no attention to Rodney. Meanwhile no one else sat next to him either. Oh! Here came Ruby but she was with a bunch of girls. They got on the bus all laughing and giggling. Ruby said hi to him but sat across the aisle with one of her friends, the others sitting close by. Hector was burning inside; he could feel his face getting red. *Why wouldn't she sit with him?* he thought. He needed her so he could look good! The doors closed and the bus started to move. He thought maybe she would move over to his side but she didn't...she was in a conversation with the other girls. His heart sank. He turned around to see where

Rodney sat when he saw the loud mouth boy whispering something to another boy. They both laughed. Hector knew they were talking about Rodney. Again, he felt bad for him, but didn't want to put himself in the position to be a target too. He turned around and minded his own business.

Ruby's mom promised she would not be waiting at the bus stop when she got home. Ruby thought she was too old for that now. Hector's mom was waiting there though. They both got off the bus, and the bus zoomed away taking the others to their own homes. Hector wondered how far away Rodney lived.

Hector's mom was anxious to hear about his day, but he was not in the mood to talk. He kept wondering why Ruby didn't sit with him. They said good bye and Ruby ran up the walk way to her house hoping for a good snack, she was hungry! She had no idea that Hector was upset. Ruby felt like she had a good day, even met some new friends, she couldn't wait to tell her mom all about it. She wondered how Hector's day went and decided that maybe later she would take Bonnet for a walk over to his house to talk about their first day. She hoped he made a few new friends. She had seen Andrea, but Andrea did not speak to her.

Chapter Twenty-Two

"I'm hommme," Ruby called out as she walked into the house.

Her mom was in the kitchen cutting up some fruit for Ruby's after school snack. She bent down to pet Bonnet who was excited to see her.

"Does she need to go out mom?" Ruby asked.

"No, I just let her back in." said her mom. "How was your first day of school Ruby?"

Ruby told her all about her day and about meeting new friends from different elementary schools. She told her mom about homeroom and her locker,

"I think I'm going to like this school, mom." Ruby said.

Her mom was happy to hear it. She asked how Hector did and if she saw Andrea. Ruby told her she didn't know how Hector did, he had lunch with her, but there was a whole table full of kids so she didn't really get to talk to him yet. She had a little bit of homework so she asked if after she was done with her homework, she could take Bonnet and walk over to see if Hector and talk about their day.

Hector went right to his room when he got home. His mom thought this meant that his day did not go well. She felt so bad for him and wondered what she could do about it. After a little while she took some cookies and knocked on his door. He was just lying on his bed with Ranger by his side, his best friend in the whole world. His mom sat down on the edge of the bed. She asked how his day was. He started to tell her about the guides and his locker and homeroom teacher, and everything sounded ok so far. His mom wondered what was bothering Hector.

"Did you make any new friends today, Hector?"

Then he started to tell her about Rodney and how he did nothing when the bullying started. Hector was feeling really guilty and just all around bad about himself. His mom had to think about what to say, I mean what would you do? It sounds good to say that you would step up and be his friend, but if you were really in that situation, what would you do?

"Hector, you're not a bad person for wanting to be part of the popular crowd; everyone wants that, to be liked and included...everyone would want that, but not at the expense of others. You never want to purposely hurt someone, because then you will feel the hurt of your own conscience, and it's just not right." His mom said.

"What's a conscience?" Hector asked.

"Your conscience is that feeling inside you that lets you know if you treated someone badly or if you did something you know is wrong. It just makes you feel like something is not right. It can be very uncomfortable. It looks like your conscience is telling you that you treated someone badly, is that right?"

"Well, I didn't exactly treat him badly, I just ignored what was happening to him because I was afraid that they would start on me if I said or did anything to make it look like he was my friend."

"Well," said his mom, "that is a tough situation. And a hard decision to make right in the moment without thinking about it. Think about what happened with you and Ruby and Andrea. What did Ruby do?" his mom asked.

"She stuck up for me," said Hector. "But that's different because Ruby is already popular, you should see all the friends she has, mom! She didn't even sit with me on the way home from school!" he whined.

Oh boy, his mom thought, *he really did have a hard day and he didn't even get bullied.* "Hector, you have to think about your day and decide what kind of person you want to be. Did you like Rodney before all this started?"

"Yes," said Hector with his head hanging low. He did think Rodney would make a good friend.

"Sometimes being in the popular crowd looks better than it really is. You have to learn how to just be ok with who you are and how you want to treat others. I think Ruby would have been ok with having Andrea and you as a friend, but it didn't work out that way. I'm sure she's upset over losing her friend, but if she would have taken on Andrea's behavior and stood against you, then her conscience probably would be bothering her. Don't you think? And how would you have felt if that had happened Hector?" his mom asked.

Hector had to think about that for a minute. He never thought of it that way. I guess he was just thinking of his own feelings and not others. Hector was looking like he might cry. Growing up was really hard to do sometimes. There's a lot to think about. Hector suddenly wished he had Rodney's phone number. Did he need to apologize to Rodney? He could have sat with Rodney on the bus for the ride home instead of sitting alone feeling rejected by Ruby. *I think*

Ruby was right, thought Hector, *having lots of friends is a good thing.*

He said to his mom, "Ruby told me it's good to have lots of friend's mom. She has popular friends and not so popular friends and they don't seem to mind each other. How does she do that?"

"It's hard to say Hector, maybe you should talk to Ruby about it. Why don't you give her a call?"

Hector called Ruby and asked her to come over. Ruby was already getting her shoes on to walk Bonnet over to see him, she told him she'd be right over.

Bonnet was getting a little better at walking on a leash but still liked to run a bit, so Ruby got to Hector's in no time at all. When Hector answered the door, Bonnet and Ranger were happy to see each other too. She let her off the leash and the two of them wrestled around a little bit before running off to do whatever dogs do when they visit a friend. Ruby and Hector went into the family room, he asked her if she wanted to play video games but Ruby just wanted to talk about their day. They told each other about their teachers and their locker and then Hector wanted to get Ruby's input about what happened with Rodney.

"Ruby, I'm sure you probably know that I was bullied a lot at my old school."

"Yes," Ruby said, "you've told me that before, did it happen today?"

"No," said Hector, "but someone next to me that I started to talk to got tripped in homeroom and he fell into me. He told me he was sorry for falling into me, but I ignored him because I was afraid that they would do the same thing to me. I was so glad up to then that nobody bothered me and thought I might even be one of the popular kids this year in my new school, so I didn't want to ruin that. I wanted to know how you do it, Ruby. How do you be friends with people that are popular and the ones that are not?" Hector hung his head while asking Ruby this important question. He was ashamed of his behavior but still wanted to be one of the popular kids. He didn't want to be bullied everyday again.

"Hector, I don't think of myself as popular. I like all kinds of friends. Each one has a different way about them that I like. I don't know why I don't get bullied, but I'm not sure what to do either when that happens in front of me. Sometimes I will stick up for someone and sometimes I just walk away. I know I should always stick up for them; I'm not sure why I don't. Sometimes I can just make a joke of it and get that person away from them. If you like Rodney, then you should be his friend."

"I know," said Hector, "but I'm scared, I don't want it to be like last year and the year before and the year before."

"Well I think if you don't take a chance and make a friend no matter what others think of them, then you will feel like this all the time." Ruby answered. "It doesn't look like you like feeling like this."

Hector was so confused. He still didn't know what to do. Ruby changed the subject and started to tell Hector about her locker and how hard it was to open at first but now she thinks she can do it the first time. Hector shared his experience with his locker too and they just shared their day with each other. He did not tell her he was upset that she didn't sit with him. He would have to figure that out himself. Why did it have to be so hard? Why couldn't everyone just like each other?

Chapter Twenty-Three

The next morning Hector got up still feeling confused, he kept waking up during the night thinking about what Ruby had to say and what his mom said, he felt like they were right but they also didn't know how it felt to be bullied all day. They didn't know how it felt to be embarrassed and made fun of for your hair or your clothes or even your voice. It didn't seem to matter what he did last year, he got made fun of even if he tried to keep to himself. By the time he would get home, he would be so tired and feel so ashamed and sad. He couldn't figure out what was wrong with him, why did everyone seem to hate him? Rodney seemed like a good guy, why shouldn't he befriend him? He decided that he would sit near him in homeroom and get to know him a little more. Making that decision made him feel relieved but he was still nervous about getting bullied himself.

Ruby and Hector met out front to wait for the bus. Their moms stayed inside. Hector told Ruby that he was going to give Rodney a chance and try not to think about what could happen to him as a result of befriending someone who was getting bullied. She could tell he was all nervous but she felt proud of him for his decision. Here came the bus and off to school they went. Ruby sat next to a girlfriend when they got on but Hector didn't seem to mind this morning. His mind was full.

Ruby was looking forward to getting her school supplies list today. She loved to go shopping for all new folders, pens and pencils. She hoped she could find a mirror with a magnet on the back to hang in her locker. She liked summer vacation but she liked to go back to school too.

Hector was looking forward to a new day at school, but he was nervous wondering if he could actually befriend Rodney without getting bullied himself. He'd see how he felt when he got to school. Who knows his bullying might start any minute now, Loud Mouth Boy was getting on at the next stop.

Loud Mouth Boy stepped up onto the bus. He had a scowl on his face. He did not look happy. Nobody knew that he had to step through a fight between his mom and dad to get out to the bus stop on time. He had a lot of anger inside him. As he stepped onto the bus, he stopped to look at each rider. Everyone seemed to shrink in fear a little bit including Hector. Loud Mouth Boy stopped at Hector's seat and looked Hector in the eye. Hector tried not to put his head down, but to look right back at Loud Mouth Boy. He sat down next to Hector. Hector didn't know what to do, so he did nothing, just looked straight ahead like no one was sitting next to him. Loud Mouth Boy sat with his hand on the seat in front of him looking like he was going to jump up any minute. Ruby looked on to see what was going to happen. Loud Mouth Boy never bothered her, but she was still a little scared of him. She hoped Hector would be ok.

Next stop was Rodney's. Rodney and a few other kids got on the bus. Everyone was so quiet. Rodney looked at Hector, wondering what was going on. Why was everyone so quiet? And what was Hector doing sitting with the big bully? Did he try to friend a bully yesterday? Rodney went to the middle of the bus and sat down. Loud Mouth Boy must have forgotten about yesterday when he tripped Rodney in homeroom, he didn't even seem to notice him or anyone else. He just looked really angry and said nothing to no one. It seemed like a long ride to school that day.

When they arrived at school, Loud Mouth Boy did not get up and so Hector just sat there and waited. He was scared. When everyone was off the bus, Loud Mouth Boy got up and walked off the bus like he was on a mission. A mission to do what, Hector did not know, but he didn't want to be in his way, that was for sure!

When they got to homeroom, Loud Mouth Boy went to the back of the room to be with his "friends." As he went by desks, he shoved books and backpacks to the floor. The teacher was out in the hallway. The kids did not know whether or not to bend over and pick up their belongings so they just sat in their seats and were very quiet. When Mr. Fink came in and it was so quiet, he looked around in disbelief. Then he noticed all the books and backpacks on the floor. He had heard ahead of school that Loud Mouth Boy was a problem in whatever class he was in so he thought he knew what happened.

"Anybody care to tell me why all this stuff is on the floor?" Mr. Fink asked.

Nobody said a word, but there were snickers from behind Loud Mouth Boy. His friends nervously giggled and snickered.

"Mr. Jackson..." Mr. Fink said. (Loud Mouth Boy's real name is Ryan Jackson) "Are you responsible for this mess?"

"Uh, now why would you think that?" Loud Mouth Boy said sarcastically as he turned around to smile at his friends. His friends snickered a little louder as if to support him.

"I think you are going to pick up all those books and backpacks and put them back on the desks they came from, RIGHT NOW." Mr. Fink said sternly.

"I'm not pickin' up nothing." Loud Mouth replied.

"You're going to pick it up or you will go to the principal's office!"

"Well, I've never met the principal yet, I guess the second day of school is a good time for that meeting." Said Loud Mouth. It didn't look like this bothered him at all. He actually seemed to be enjoying himself. His friends behind him looked a little nervous, but were still supporting Loud Mouth Boy.

Mr. Fink walked to the back of the room and took Loud Mouth Boy by the arm and led him out of the room. Loud Mouth went willingly with a big smile on his face waving at the class like he was going on vacation.

The class seemed to let out a breath of relief when Mr. Fink took the bully out of the room. Loud Mouth's friends however, were very quiet. They didn't know how to act once their "leader" was gone.

Chapter Twenty-Four

Mr. Fink did not let go of Ryan's arm the whole way to the principal's office, Ryan kept laughing and saying things like, "Ohhhh, I'm so scared of the big bad principal."

Mr. Fink said nothing to him, just kept walking. When they got to the principal's office, Mr. Fink walked Ryan right in and told him to sit down. Ryan did as he was told. He did not look worried at all. Mr. Scott had heard lots of stories about Ryan's behavior in elementary school.

"What did you do this time Ryan? I thought maybe we could start out the year in your new school in a more positive way," said Mr. Scott. "I hoped we would not have to meet like this on the second day."

Hmmm, he knows me on the second day? thought Ryan, *I must be famous.* And he puffed out his chest like he was proud of himself.

Mr. Fink explained what happened in homeroom. Ryan just sat there and smiled.

"Shall I call your mother Ryan? What should we do with you? What do you suggest? How can we make this a better year?" Mr. Scott asked.

"Go ahead and call her, do you think she's going to care? Just do with me whatever you want, but don't send me home," said Ryan

"Well if you don't want to be here and you don't want to be at home, where do you want to be?"

"I don't know, the Army, the Navy, anywhere away from here," Ryan said sarcastically. He just knew that the last time he got suspended from school, it didn't go well for him at home.

Mr. Scott secretly thought the Army or Navy would be a good place for Ryan, but he is just a young boy, 12 years old. There had to be a solution, and he was determined to find it. He also heard that Ryan was a smart boy that didn't apply himself to his work. He wondered what his home life was like. Mr. Scott decided that the school counselor needed to be a part of this. Maybe she could help, but in the meantime, Ryan needed some consequences for his behavior. Mr. Scott told Ryan that he would be going to detention for a whole week.

He would have to stay after school and take the late bus home. He would also have extra work to keep him busy in detention. He told him to stay seated while he went to talk to Mrs. Grace, the school counselor. She might have some solutions to get this kid on a better track.

Mr. Fink had to get back to his class, so the secretary came in and sat at Mr. Scott's desk while he was gone. Ryan sat with his head down as if to ignore everyone around him.

Mrs. Grace wanted to help. She suggested he come to her office every day for lunch for a while. She called it the Lunch Bunch. She tried to gather some of the troubled kids for a short time during the day to give them extra attention. So, Mr. Scott agreed to start out with that, but Ryan would still have detention for a week. He would be her first guest in Lunch Bunch.

Ryan was not excited about this news. *Eating lunch with a teacher?* he thought... *How lame.* It was decided that Mr. Scott would not call his mother. He thought they would give the Lunch Bunch a try and see if that worked out for the good. Mr. Scott gave Ryan a pass and sent him back to class. Homeroom was over by this time and so he went to his first class. Most of his classmates were not happy to see him back, but his little pack of followers was glad to have their "leader" back and wondered what would be next. They thought Ryan made the school day more fun.

Ryan walked in like he owned the place a few minutes late. Smiling while he took a seat near the back of the room, one of the other bullies whispered loudly to him, "Heeey Ryyaan, how was the principal's office? Are you getting kicked out of school again?" The others snickered.

Ryan just looked at him and told him to shut up. The kid sat back in his seat and didn't say another word. The teacher told Ryan to come up front and sit. He did not like sitting in the front but he went. Ryan was quiet for the whole class.

He was thinking about lunchtime when he would be spending time with that lame counselor. Meanwhile Mr. Fink went to all of his other teachers to warn them of his disruptive behavior so they could be aware of it before the class even started.

The teacher for the second class of the day decided to try to stop things before they even started, so she made a seating chart and put Ryan in the front row. He sure did not like that and let it be known. He was complaining how lame it was, but she ignored his protests. She would watch how class went to see if she needed to spread out any of the other kids. Hector was seated next to Rodney. Ryan was next to Rodney on the other side.

It seemed to Hector that this might be a better year. The worst bully was out of the back of the room now and closer to the teacher so she could keep an eye on what he was doing. It brought him closer to Hector though, and that bothered him a little bit. The seating arrangement didn't help the time between classes though. The bell rang and Hector went to his locker to grab his notebook for the next class. Ryan came up behind him and slammed his locker shut almost on Hector's hand, leered at him and kept walking, slamming others lockers as he went. *Ugh*, thought Hector, *why does school have to be so stressful?* This loud mouth boy didn't seem to single anyone out, he seemed to bully everyone. He wondered how Ruby would handle this.

Lunch time came and Ryan thought he would be able to just go to lunch and forget about lunch with the counselor, but she was waiting for him outside of class to walk him down to her office. The kids in his class were all watching with curiosity, wondering what was happening. None of them had met Mrs. Grace yet, so they didn't know who she was or where she was taking Ryan. He just looked back at them with a grin and then ducked his head down.

"I don't have a lunch," said Ryan miserably without looking at Mrs. Grace.

"We'll stop at the cafeteria and you can buy, do you have money?"

"No," said Ryan.

"I'm sure they will give you a lunch today, but make sure you bring money for lunch from now on, or pack one."

"Yeah, right," said Ryan under his breath. Did she really think that was going to happen? Ryan used to just steal parts of other kids lunches last year. His parents did not hand out money and what was he to pack?

Mrs. Graces' office had a desk, a table with a few chairs around it, lots of books and a chalk board. Mrs. Grace invited Ryan to have a seat at the table with his lunch and she set her packed lunch down across the table from him. *Looks like she's going to sit right with me,* thought Ryan. *Ugh, why can't they just leave me alone? I'm NOT talking.*

"So, Ryan, tell me a little about you and your family." Mrs. Grace thought she would start out with a little background information. She heard about what a trouble maker he was from Mr. Scott, his previous school sent along his records.

Ryan said nothing. He just sat there staring at his lunch. He was hungry but he didn't want to give this teacher the satisfaction of thinking this was going to work. His stomach was growling and he couldn't control it though, and Mrs.

Grace noticed. *This is going to be a tough one,* thought Mrs. Grace.

"If you don't eat your lunch, your stomach is going to be growling even louder when you get back to class Ryan, come on, you don't have to talk today, just try to eat a little bit." Mrs. Grace figured she would give him a few days to get used to her and eventually he would start talking. She just had to have some patience.

After about ten minutes of listening to his stomach growling, Ryan picked at his lunch until the entire tray was empty of food. When the bell rang, he got up to leave.

"Hold on Ryan, you wait until I excuse you before you leave." Mrs. Grace said.

He rolled his eyes and just stood there.

"Have a seat please." She told him sternly.

Ryan backed up and sat down in his chair hard. Mrs. Grace waited a minute and then said, "You may go to your next class now, Ryan. Will you come on your own tomorrow, or do I need to be waiting for you after class?"

He said nothing, just walked out the door. Mrs. Grace knew she would be meeting him at his class for a few days. She wondered if he would have a lunch with him tomorrow. She was glad he was the only Lunch Buncher at this time. He was going to take some one-on-one time for sure.

Hector was hungry! He couldn't wait to get to lunch. When he walked in, he saw Rodney sitting alone again. This time he went over to him and asked if he could sit with him. Rodney looked at him with a puzzled look on his face. He couldn't figure Hector out so he just nodded and moved his stuff aside. Hector looked over at Ruby's table. She was looking at him, smiling. That made Hector feel better, but he was still unsure of what to talk about and how to start. Rodney waited.

"So," Hector started, "how do you like school so far Rodney?"

Rodney hesitated for a minute and then said, "Well, it didn't start out too good."

"I was glad to see that loud mouth kid taken out of class today, weren't you?" Hector asked.

"Yeah, but for how long will that work. I'm glad the teacher put him up front but did she have to put him next to me? Maybe I'll move to the back again."

Soon Hector and Rodney were talking like old friends. Rodney told Hector that he liked to play the guitar. Hector always wanted to play an instrument, this year he would have that chance, he just had to decide what to play. Rodney said he'd never join the band. He was afraid to play in front of anyone, especially at school. Hector told him about solving the Rubik's cube and Rodney seemed very interested. They exchanged phone numbers just before the bell rang and walked back to class together.

Chapter Twenty-Five

Ryan didn't care if he had detention. It was a new thing for him; they didn't have it in elementary school. At least he didn't have to go right home, and, *they won't miss me anyways.* Ryan thought. The first day of detention he had math sheets to work on. Pretty simple when he looked at it, thinking about whether he should actually do it. He was pretty bored, but school work? No thanks. The first day he put his name on it that was all. He put his head down on his arms and tried to take a little nap. The next day when he got there, the same sheet was waiting for him with his name on it. He sat there staring at the paper. It seemed like the teachers at this school were a little harder than elementary school was. It seemed like they were ganging up on him, *who's the bully now,* he thought with a scowl. He was the only one in detention. Was he the only one who got in trouble in this school or what? *Lame, lame, lame,* he thought.

Ryan picked up the pencil that they also placed on the desk, and started to do the problems. He was done with it in a few minutes. What to do with the rest of the hour.... hmmm.

He turned the paper over and started to doodle different designs. He looked up at the teacher in charge of detention and wondered if she was as bored as him. She was reading a book... *How boring*, he thought. Ryan didn't like to read either. All school work was boring to him. Before the hour was up, he sketched a picture of the teacher on the back of his worksheet. Thinking nothing of it, he turned it in before leaving to catch the late bus home.

Mrs. Grace was keeping track of Ryan's detention. She had asked his teachers for worksheets to keep him busy while in detention. She also wanted to see what his level of understanding was for each subject. When she received the math sheet and noticed that all the answers were right, she was surprised, but when she turned it over, she was really surprised! The details in the drawing were so good. There was definitely more to this kid than met the eye. Maybe a little encouragement would be one of the things to help him.

Chapter Twenty-Six

The next morning, Hector and Rodney walked into homeroom together. Ryan was still out at his locker. The rest of Ryan's friends were already in their seats being a little loud as they made fun of everyone who came in the door, including Rodney and Hector.

"Ooohhh, here come the two boyfriends.... how cute," one said, sarcastically.

Hector and Rodney both looked at each other and just kept walking to their seats like they hadn't heard them. The teacher was out in the hall welcoming the kids as they came in. Ryan walked in and wacked both Hector and Rodney in the head as he walked by. They sat like nothing happened, while the bully's in the back of the room laughed and talked more about them. The other kids were silent, probably afraid of it happening to them.

Mr. Fink walked into the classroom just in time to hear the tail end of the bunch of bully's laughing and making fun of Hector and Rodney. Ryan for once was not involved in that, but he was looked up to and so they were showing off for him. Mr. Fink was learning more about his students every morning. He knew who the bullies were and who was getting bullied. As soon as they seen Mr. Fink, they all stopped at once and it was so quiet in there. He closed the door, took attendance and they all stood for the Pledge of Allegiance. Once they were all sitting down again, they began chatting with each other. Mr. Fink called attention.

"It has come to my attention that there is some bullying going on here in homeroom. Not a good way to start the day, folks. If you don't like someone, it's ok, but you don't need to make fun of them or try to hurt them. I won't have it in my homeroom. If I notice anything from now on, there will be assigned seats and no talking at all to start the day. Understood?" Mr. Fink said. He looked at each student one at a time to make sure they listened and understood the new rule. Ryan just rolled his eyes. *What's with this school he thought?*

While walking to the first class, Hector and Rodney were talking about Mr. Fink thinking he was a good teacher and hoped that homeroom would be better from now on. Suddenly both Hector and Rodney went flying into the lockers. Their books were knocked out of their arms by hitting into each other. Thankfully neither of them fell to the floor, but it was bad enough.

One of the bullies from the back of the room winked at them and hurried on down the hall. The other kids walked around them like garbage on the ground. The boys bent over to pick up their books and move on so they wouldn't be late. Hector and Rodney looked at each other with no words. Both felt such shame and sadness...there really was no words for them, just more tears on the inside. Both were glad for the assigned seats in first period. Hector couldn't help but wonder if he should have befriended Rodney. Would things have worked out differently? His hopes of being popular this year were shattering more and more every day.

Seven more years of this? *I hate school*, thought Hector, when in reality, it wasn't school he hated; it was the way he was treated in school. They were the last ones into first period class. Both felt like everyone was staring at them and thinking what losers they were as they took their seat. Papers were sticking out of their books from being knocked to the floor. Both boys were still a little flustered. Does anyone deserve to be treated like this? How could they even learn anything with this going on? The first period class was history. At the end of class, the teacher assigned homework for the week. It was to write a history of themselves. *Oh great,* thought Hector sarcastically, *this ought to be fun.*   They had a week to get it done. Hector wondered what she was going to do with the completed essays. He hoped they would not have to read them to the class, some teachers liked to do that, make you get up in front of the class and speak.   It was so humiliating and stressful when that happened. He decided right then that no matter what; he would not be getting up in front of the class to read his.

Soon it was lunch time.   Ruby knew that Hector was having a hard time in school, so she decided to invite him and Rodney to join her and her friends for lunch. Hector wasn't sure this was a good idea. He was afraid of the other kids making fun of him in front of all her friends and embarrassing not only himself, but her. She insisted so Hector and Rodney joined the table and Ruby introduced them to her friends. They all seemed to welcome them in a good manner, but Hector still didn't trust it. Hector and Rodney didn't say much at lunch, and nobody really gave them much attention. Surprisingly, lunch went ok and Hector started to relax a little bit. Ryan was no longer in lunch but his friends were. They were a pretty loud table off in the corner.   He hoped they stayed there.   He wondered where Ryan went for lunch, he seen him in the lunch line but after that he was gone. As long as he was gone it was ok with him.

Mrs. Grace met Ryan at his class again today. She smiled at him and greeted him, but he just rolled his eyes and put his head down and followed her to the lunch line. He saw all his friends at a table in the corner. He wanted to join them but that wasn't going to be happening any time soon. They all got noisy when they saw him, waving at him and even teasing/bullying him a little bit. Here was their leader being led around the school by some teacher. What was going on? Again, he had no money, but Mrs. Grace talked to the lunch lady and they gave him lunch again. She would have to take care of that matter later in the day. They had a special fund for kids with no lunch money and she would get him enrolled in it today. They went back to her office and sat at the table. Again, Ryan just sat slouched down with is head hanging down.

"Come on Ryan, let's not do this every day, just eat your lunch and then we'll talk a little bit." Mrs. Grace said a little sternly.

Ryan grunted, "UGH," he said, "How long do I have to come here?"

"Well, time will tell, Ryan, the sooner you drop the tough guy act and talk to me, the sooner you'll be back in the lunch room, so it's up to you."

Ryan picked up his fork and started to eat his French Fries. *This lady will not give up,* thought Ryan. He was pretty hungry though, he hardly ever had anything for breakfast at home.

"So, tell me a little bit about your family, Ryan." Mrs. Grace started.

Ryan just looked at her. *Why is she bothering with me? Why does she want to know about my family? She probably won't believe me anyways. Why doesn't she just give it up?* he thought.

"I have a mother and a father. That's my family, the end," Ryan said in his tough guy voice not bothering to lift his head or sit up straighter.

"Where does your dad work? Does your mom work?" Mrs. Grace just wanted the basics; she wasn't asking hard questions. She kept her voice patient.

"My dad doesn't work. My mom works at Walmart. Why do you want to know this? Just let me go back to lunch, will ya?"

Mrs. Grace pulled out his math worksheet. She praised him on getting the answers all right. That got a little spark of energy from Ryan. He was not used to being praised. Then she turned the paper over and looked at the drawing he did of the detention teacher. "Wow!" she said, "this is some drawing Ryan!" She could tell that he was liking the praise. He started to sit up a little straighter as he looked at her to make sure she wasn't going to suddenly put him down like he was used to.

"I think we should get you into some art classes so you can show some of this talent off, it's great!" Mrs. Grace continued. She went to her desk and pulled up his schedule on her computer. "We have an after-school art club you could join, Ryan, then there's a late bus home, would you like that?" He still didn't trust her. She said, "Why don't you think about it and let me know." He said nothing.

The bell rang and this time Ryan didn't move. He waited until she told him it was ok to go. Mrs. Grace smiled and told him she'd see him tomorrow. *Progress,* she thought, *progress.*

Ryan went back to class feeling a little odd. He couldn't figure out why he felt kinda good about his lunch today, but that good feeling didn't last because his buddies were waiting for him and it was back to bully mode. They were all laughing and hitting each other in the shoulders, shoving and pushing a little bit, just for the fun of it.

"Heyyyy, here comes Ryan, where were you Ryan, having lunch with that lame teacher?" one of the guys sarcastically slurred.

Ryan gave him a dirty look and walked past all of them into the class. The others were laughing and joking around. They were starting to have a louder mouth than him. Something was changing in Ryan and he felt confused. As he walked by Hector, he resisted the urge to knock his books off his desk or whack him in the head...probably better off since the teacher was in the room.

Chapter Twenty-Seven

Hector and Ruby couldn't wait to get home. It was such a nice fall day and both were ready for some explore time in the woods. When they got off the bus, they made some plans to get together in a little while. Ruby had to take care of Bonnet and of course she wanted to have a snack before they went. Hector was feeling tired out from all the bullying he put up with during the day but didn't say anything to Ruby about it, a hike in the woods would probably make him feel better, especially with Ruby.

The hike into the woods was good for both of them. The fallen leaves were crunchy under their feet and it was just the right temperature, not too hot and not too cold, just right. As they walked along, they started talking about their day. Ruby knew from other friends that Hector was getting bullied a lot, along with his new friend, Rodney. Ruby had heard that Mrs. Grace, the guidance counselor, was someone that helped when you had a problem. She thought that if Hector went to her, she might be able to help him. Hector tried to explain to her that if he "tells" it gets worse.

"But maybe you could ask for help without telling," Ruby said.

Hector couldn't see how that could happen, but he started thinking about it. He didn't know how to go about getting to see her or who to ask about it. He heard that Ryan was having lunch with her, along with his detention for pushing all the books off the desks. His detention would be over tomorrow, but he didn't know how long the lunches would go on. What could Mrs. Grace do for him? He wondered, and how could he get to see her? He decided that he would stop by her office in the morning before homeroom. Maybe this school would be different.

Ruby and Hector were having so much fun, they started out on the tire swing, taking turns swinging While Hector was swinging, Ruby was trying to climb a tree and she managed to get up on one branch when Hector was done swinging. Ranger was with them too; he was just scouting around doing a lot of sniffing. Suddenly Ranger started digging and barking. Both Ruby and Hector ran over to see what he was barking and digging about. By the time they got to him, he had uncovered a nest of baby bunnies! Oh, they were so cute! Ruby just wanted to pick one up and hold it, but Hector told her that wasn't a good idea. They should really just cover them back up and leave them be. The mom bunny's left the little ones hidden during the day; she would be back he told her. They decided to go throw rocks in the pond for a while. Ruby could make them skip, she wondered if Hector could do it too. They gathered some rocks and went to the edge of the pond. Neither one of them had their rain boots on so they were being very careful. As they were skipping rocks, a big fish jumped out of the water.

"WOW!" exclaimed Hector. "I'll bet that's the same fish I caught and put back! He grew!"

They just had all kinds of fun that day and Hector felt happier than he had all week. Why did he have to go back to school? He hoped this Mrs. Grace would be able to help him and Rodney. They just wanted to go to school without being picked on every single day. Hector wouldn't even go to the bathroom all day because he was afraid to go into the boy's lavatory. At the other school, he had his head pushed into the toilet. Then they called him toilet head all day, he couldn't wait to get home and take a shower. He didn't tell his mom what happened that day, he was too embarrassed even for his mom. Every day he wondered what was wrong with him, why, when they didn't even know him, didn't anybody like him? What was wrong with him?

Chapter Twenty-Eight

While Ruby and Hector waited for the bus that next morning, they talked about him going to see Mrs. Grace. Hector was really nervous about it, he was afraid to speak up, but he knew he didn't want to continue every day getting bullied. It only gets worse; he knew that from experience. Ruby encouraged him and told him if he wanted her to come with him, she would, but he knew he needed to go alone or with Rodney. He had talked to Rodney on the phone last night and told him of his plan. Rodney needed to think about it overnight to decide whether he would go with Hector to talk with Mrs. Grace.

The next bus stop was for Ryan. Hector always dreaded this pick up and as usual Ryan was loud and in charge when he stepped onto the bus, telling everyone he had "arrived." Like he was the king or something. On his way past Hector he whacked him in the head with the back of his hand and then laughed. Ruby happened to see this and spoke up, "Hey! Not nice! How would you like it if someone hit you like that?"

"Oh, did you want a back hand too?" Ryan quietly hissed at her so the bus driver would not hear him.

Ruby was not quiet. "So now you're going to start hitting girls, is it another bad habit of yours?" She said loudly.

The bus driver looked in his big mirror and loudly told everyone to quiet down, he didn't want no trouble. Ryan smiled at Ruby and took his seat in the back with his friends who were enjoying the whole scene. Hector sat with his head down. Ruby meant well, but she might have just made it worse for him. The bus was slowing down for Rodney's pick up. As soon as he stepped up onto the bus, Ryan and his friends started clapping and yelling, "Yay! It's Rod-Face, it's Rod-Face," they laughed and were having such a good time. Rodney quickly slid into his seat next to Hector. He looked over at Hector and whispered, "I'll go with you." Both boys were quiet for the rest of the ride. Ruby was fuming. She thought she just might go into Mrs. Grace's office herself!

Hector and Rodney got into homeroom before Ryan and his buddy's, they both chickened out going to Mrs. Grace's office. He hoped it was a good thing that they got in first until Ryan kicked Hector's desk and pretended to almost fall. When Mr. Fink looked up, Ryan started yelling that Hector tripped him. Mr. Fink looked at Hector who was looking a little, or I should say, a lot surprised and scared.

"Did you stick your foot out and trip Ryan?" Mr. Fink asked Hector.

Hector had his head down. Mr. Fink knew darn well that Ryan faked the trip, if anything Hector tried to avoid Ryan. He knew who the bully's in this class were.

Hector was not sure how to answer the question. If he said yes, he would be punished by Mr. Fink. If he said no, then Ryan was sure to get back at him in the hallways somehow. Hector was saying nothing, so Mr. Fink asked the class, "did anyone see Hector stick his foot out and trip Ryan as he walked past his desk?" No one said a word. The whole class just looked down at their desks. They knew not to get involved. Some were on the bus this morning when Ruby spoke up and wondered what was going to happen to her for speaking up.

Mr. Fink thought for a few moments before he decided to send Hector down to Mrs. Grace. He made it look like Hector was the one in trouble. Mr. Fink thought that maybe Mrs. Grace could give him a few ideas on how to handle the bullying. He'd like to see it gone completely from school, but that was not likely to happen. He gave Hector a pass and sent him down. Hector had some mixed feelings about this. Here he was planning on going to see Mrs. Grace, chickened out and now he's going because he was told to by a teacher. He knocked on her office door.

"Come in please," Mrs. Grace called out. Hector hesitantly walked in. "Have a seat Hector."

What??? How did she know my name, thought Hector! Hector didn't know it but Mr. Fink had already talked to Mrs. Grace about what was going on in his homeroom. After Hector left homeroom to go to her office, Mr. Fink called her and let her know he was coming. Hector felt like his hands were sweating, he was so nervous. Was he in trouble? He never got in trouble in school, as a matter of fact, he felt invisible as far as teachers went. He was very quiet in class and thought only the bully's noticed him. He silently took a seat across from Mrs. Grace, he glanced around her office and noticed how neat it was. There was a table and chairs and books, but everything was in its place.

"So, Hector, what brings you here?"

Hector started to stutter. He hadn't done that in a long time! "M M Mr. F F F ink sent me da da down he he here," Hector stuttered. He just didn't know how to stop it now.

"Let's slow down and find out what's happening for you, no need to be afraid Hector."

Hector wasn't sure why, but he felt like he could trust her, so for the next half hour, Hector slowly but surely told Mrs. Grace what's been going on. He also mentioned Rodney's name. She already knew that from talking to Mr. Fink, but she didn't let him know that. Next thing he knew, he missed first period class. Mrs. Grace decided that he and Rodney should come to the Lunch Bunch. Hector knew that Ryan was already coming so he couldn't see that that would help in any way, but he did trust her and didn't really know anything about this Lunch Bunch thing. Rodney would be with him too, so how bad could it be? Mrs. Grace knew that she wouldn't have to pick them up at their class so she just told him and Rodney to come to her office with their lunch, she would notify Rodney's teacher to relay the message. Hector was afraid to tell Rodney! What did he get them into? Lunch with a teacher? He had a feeling this was going to get him nothing more than more bullied.

Rodney couldn't believe his ears. "Have lunch with a teacher AND Ryan? Are you nuts??"

Hector told Rodney that for some reason he trusted Mrs. Grace and so she must have something in mind that was going to help. In the end Rodney was willing to give it a try. If they just let things go on like they were, things were bound to get worse.

The bell rang and it was time for lunch. Lunch Bunch for them. Rodney and Hector looked at each other with a knowing glance. They gathered their books and headed to their lockers to get their packed lunch. Mrs. Grace was at the door waiting for Ryan, and she did not give away that they would all be together. When they got to her office she still wasn't there yet because she and Ryan had to stop in the lunch room to pick up lunch for Ryan, so they stood around by the door as other students passed by. Ruby came by and Hector told her what happened. She was glad that he got to talk to Mrs. Grace, but was also surprised that they would be having lunch with Ryan too. She couldn't wait to hear about this.

Mrs. Grace and Ryan came down the hall. Ruby scooted off to lunch. When Ryan saw Hector and Rodney, he stopped. Mrs. Grace stopped with him and explained they would have two extra Lunch Bunchers today. Ryan did not look happy. He could not figure out this school. Why on earth would those two losers be here for lunch too? Because Hector "tripped him" in homeroom? *Ugh, this keeps getting lamer by the minute,* thought Ryan as he brushed past the two "losers" on the way into the room. He was just getting comfortable with Mrs. Grace and now these two barge in? What the heck?

Chapter Twenty-Nine

Lunch was a little awkward that first day at Lunch Bunch. Mrs. Grace knew she didn't have to introduce them to each other but she did anyways. Ryan was just staring at them with eyes that looked like daggers.

"I understand that you three have had some problems getting along since school started. Lunch Bunch is a chance to take some time out of your day and have a peaceful lunch and maybe discuss what may be bothering you." Mrs. Grace explained to them what Lunch Bunch was all about. "…and there may be others joining us in the future. First, we will all get to know each other and so while we are having lunch each of us will share a little bit about ourselves. I'll go first."

Ryan rolled his eyes.

Mrs. Grace started telling them about herself and why she loved her job. She told them that she had 2 children, both girls and both in elementary school. She knew that none of the three were going to volunteer any information about themselves unless she asked them questions.

"Ryan, why don't you start by telling us a little about your family? Do you have brothers and sisters, a dog?"

Ryan thought about not answering, but then he thought if he cooperated a little bit, he might just get out of this Lunch Bunch garbage.

"I already told you, I have a mother and a father, the end."

"How about you Hector? Can you tell us a little about your family?" Mrs. Grace asked.

Hector hoped he would not stutter, but he could not control it, and he was nervous. "I I I ha ha have a a a m m mom, and a a a da da dad. I I I ha ha have a d d dog n n named R R Ranger." Hector was sweating. It felt like the longest sentence he ever spoke. He looked up to see Ryan with a smirk on his face, he put his head down and continued to eat even though he lost his appetite. Rodney felt bad for him, he never heard him stuttering like that.

"Ok, thanks Hector, how about you Rodney, who's in your family?" Mrs. Grace asked.

Rodney was nervous too. How was he supposed to eat lunch like this? Why was he here? He didn't do anything! He felt angry. Ryan took a bite of his pizza as he looked to Rodney. It didn't look like this bothered him at all, actually he seemed to be enjoying it. Rodney was so shy they could barely hear him when he spoke, "I have a mom and dad, no pets," he practically whispered. He dreaded the rest of the day in the halls and in class with Ryan.

Mrs. Grace continued on like everything was going great. "Ok," she said, now let's share with each other our favorite thing to do." Again, Ryan rolled his eyes, and this time Mrs. Grace saw it, so she picked on him to go first. He slouched down in his seat, and stopped eating. He didn't know what to say, he had no favorite thing to do, oh wait, he liked video games. Mine Craft was his favorite, so he shared that but it sounded like he was snarling while he spoke.

Mrs. Grace asked Rodney next. His felt like his voice was still real quiet. He didn't know if he wanted Ryan to know his favorite thing to do, so he hesitated. Mrs. Grace encouraged him to share, she knew they were all struggling but she really wanted them to get to know each other. Sometimes when bullying happens the bullied and the bully could be good friends if they gave each other a chance. She hoped this could work with these three.

"I like to play my guitar," Rodney shared. He was glad he was at the table with Mrs. Grace so that Ryan would not make fun of him, but he was still thinking of the rest of the day and the bus ride home. Hector told them that he liked to play with his Rubik's Cube. His stutter was still there so it took him a few minutes to get it out. Ryan felt impatient with him and just kept staring at him.

Suddenly the bell rang and lunch was over. Rodney and Hector started to pack away their lunch stuff. They wondered why Ryan was not moving. Finally, Mrs. Grace told them all that they were excused. Rodney and Hector were nervous about the rest of the day. They thought once they stepped outside of this office, it would start, but Ryan just went on ahead of them to his locker to get his books for the next class. He didn't even look at them. They were still waiting for it though.

After a few weeks of Lunch Bunch the boys were starting to share more freely and Hector's stutter was improving each day. Ryan was not bothering them as much, but his friends seemed to keep it up. Ryan was so interested in Rodney's guitar playing, he always wanted to try it, but his parents didn't think it was a good idea so he just stopped asking. Ryan was also curious about the Rubik's Cube, but he sure didn't want either one of these losers to know that he was interested in anything they did. Talking about it at lunch was different than seeing them outside of school, how would that be? he wondered.

Chapter Thirty

Ryan was quiet the rest of the day. His friends were confused, but Ryan didn't even interact with them, he just kept to himself. He wondered what it would be like to be like Hector and Rodney. He wondered what it was like to live in their house. Oh, they were losers for sure, but there was something about them that made him quiet. He watched them in class and on the bus that day. They kept waiting for "it," but "it" didn't happen. Ryan dreaded going home. He never knew what it was going to be like when he walked in the door. His father drank so much, he couldn't understand it, and it made him so mean, why would he keep drinking? And his mom, it seemed like she would fight with him on purpose. Ryan used to sneak in the kitchen when his father stepped out for a minute and poor his beer down the drain. When he got caught, he'd really get in trouble. His father would hit him and yell at him about how much money he just poured down the drain and finally get sent to his room. He would be glad to be sent to his room because the hitting and yelling would stop and he would be in his own space, away from those two crazy people he called his parents. Did everyone live like this?

The bus came to a stop in front of Hector's house. Ryan listened to Rodney tell Hector he'd call him later and maybe Hector could come to his house. He wondered what they would do. What do you do when you go over to a friend's house? He could never invite anyone over to his house; it would be too embarrassing for them to witness his parents in "action." None of his friends ever invited him over or called him. Ryan didn't realize it but he was feeling so lonely. He had friends but there was a difference in his friends and Rodney and Hector, and he wasn't sure how to get a friend like that. It made him feel sad but angry. His usual response would be to do something to make their life a little miserable, but for the first time, he just felt very quiet. When Hector left the bus, Ryan got up and went and sat with Rodney. All his friends were waiting with anticipation that something was going to happen. Rodney thought for sure he was going to whack him in the head or throw his backpack to the ground, but he just sat there. Ryan felt very out of place, he didn't know what to say or how to act. When the bus came to Rodney's stop, Rodney feared he wouldn't let him out, but he got up and let him go without touching him or saying anything to him. Rodney was very confused and wondered what was up. He wasn't complaining but he felt like he was waiting for something to happen and he wanted to get it over with.

The next day, Mrs. Grace decided to see if Ryan would come on his own. She waited in her office for her Lunch Bunchers. Rodney and Hector came in first with their packed lunches.

Sure enough, Ryan came strolling in with his lunch tray. He was so hungry, it seemed like this was his best meal during the day. His mom didn't cook much; it was sort of a help yourself kinda kitchen. He wondered what the questions would be today. Part of him was looking forward to this lunch thing now, but he was fighting it, still trying to think of Rodney and Hector as losers, but he was starting to realize that he was the one that was losing. As he walked in, he looked at Hector and Rodney, "hey losers, wuzup?" he said.

Mrs. Grace was not going to stand for that. She put a stop to the rudeness right away. "Ryan! Please step back outside the door and come in with a greeting that is not rude. If you can't say something nice, don't say anything at all!"

Ryan looked shocked. He just stood there for a few moments. He wasn't used to being called on bad behavior so much. He tried to put that smirk on his face, but he just couldn't do it. He turned around and thought of just leaving and going to the lunch room, but for some reason he felt like he didn't want to miss lunch with the losers. What was wrong with him? Was he getting soft in the head? He walked back in the room and just said, "Hey…" Still the tough guy, but it was an improvement over the loser comment. Hector and Rodney felt uncomfortable.

Ryan sat down with his tray and started to eat. The other boys and Mrs. Grace unpacked their lunches too. It was quiet for a few minutes while they all started to eat; it looked like everyone was hungry today. "So, what shall we talk about today boys?" Mrs. Grace asked.

Ryan just rolled his eyes and said, "Can't we just eat today and not talk about anything? "

"We could do that Ryan, is that what you boys want too, just eat, no talking?"

They both looked up, not knowing the right answer. "It's ok with me," said Hector and Rodney nodded his head in agreement, so the four of them ate in silence that day. Mrs. Grace knew change was happening, she had talked to

Mr. Fink and he told her that things were settling down a bit in homeroom, so a silent day was ok for today. Ryan was thinking all kinds of questions in his mind but his pride would not allow him to speak up and be friendly after all the bullying he'd done so far. These two losers were turning out to be ok after all...sorta. He wanted to know about the guitar, what kind it is, and what kind of music Rodney plays. He wanted to know about the Rubik's Cube and how Hector learned to do it and would he show him some time.

When the bell rang, Mrs. Grace asked them all to stay a minute. She gave them some homework. Lunch homework? Ryan thought, what the heck? Hector and Ryan could not imagine what kind of homework you would get in lunch. Mrs. Grace wanted them each to write down two questions they would like to ask each other and bring it after the weekend. Ryan didn't think much about it, at first, he thought he would not bother with such a lame assignment, but then he remembered his questions he was thinking about in his mind while they ate in silence. Hmm, he thought, maybe this will work out. Rodney and Hector just looked at each other with a little bit of fear. Did they even want to know about Ryan? What could be a question for him...why don't you like us? What did we do? Everybody went on with their day with the idea of questions in the back of their minds. Ryan started to feel a little excited about it but didn't want to let that feeling get out of control, I mean he was the cool one here.

Chapter Thirty-One

Woo-hoo! It was the weekend! Even though Ruby had no real plans she was glad to have two days off. Everything was looking so pretty outside. The leaves were all kinds of beautiful colors and some were crunchy on the ground, she loved fall. On the bus ride home, she called out to Hector across the aisle and asked him if he wanted to go to the woods this weekend. It sounded good to Hector, but he wanted to invite Rodney along. He didn't think it would turn out like it did when Ruby invited Andrea, Rodney was not like her and he already liked Ruby. Ryan, who was sitting a few seats away from them heard them talking. Woods? What woods? Ryan was dreading the weekend. He never had anything to do except play video games and that got boring when it was just him. He wasn't sure why but he started to feel angry at them. He wanted to hurt them. He got up and went to the back of the bus where his "friends" were and started to call insults towards Ruby, Hector, and Rodney. Rodney and Hector felt like they knew it was going to happen. It was too good to be true that Ryan could be nice. Ryan's "friends" were glad to have him back and joined in on the name calling. The bus ride suddenly felt longer.

Ruby and Hector got off at their stop and talked for a few minutes. Ryan watched out the window and started saying some things about them being boyfriend and girlfriend and not very nice statements to the rest of the kids on the bus. Rodney was the next one off the bus. He felt so relieved when he stepped down onto the grass. Two days off! A break. Hector told him he'd call him to come over, and he was looking forward to that.

Ruby ran up on her porch to gather little Bonnet into her arms. She missed her when she was at school and loved the welcome home she received when she came home. Her mom had a snack ready for her and she munched on it while talking to her mom about Ryan and how he seems angry and mean at one moment and then other times he seemed to be thinking about something that makes him quiet and not so threatening.

"Ryan probably has problems of his own, Ruby, most times when a bully bully's it has something to do with their own self. He's probably angry about something that's out of his control and he can't get angry at that so he takes it out on others," her mom said. "I'm not sure what to do about it, but I bet there's a nice boy under all that anger. I'm glad your guidance counselor is taking an interest, maybe she can help."

"I hope so," said Ruby. "Hey, Mom what are we going to do tonight? Or this weekend?"

"Well, tonight I hoped to have a game and movie night. I'll make some taco's and we can play a game right after dinner and then later pop some popcorn and put a movie in, how does that sound?" her mom said.

"Sounds good Mom, what about tomorrow? I think it's going to be a nice day, a nice day for the woods?" Ruby asked with a big smile on her face.

"Tomorrow I'm going to strip beds and wash all our sheets. I want to hang them outside because they smell so good when I do that. You are free for the woods! Will Hector go with you?"

"Hector and Rodney!" Ruby said. She was looking forward to getting to know Rodney a little bit since they were not in the same class at school.

After Ruby finished her snack, she called Hector. He was ok for tomorrow too and said he'd call Rodney right away to see if he could join them. She wanted to start her homework right away so she could get it all done and not have to think about it all weekend. She hadn't jumped on her trampoline all week and she wanted to get out there and practice her flips.

The next morning Ruby jumped right out of bed, excited for the day. She had some chores to take care of first but was meeting Hector half way between their houses with their lunches packed at 11:00. Bonnet was still not able to go to the woods with them. She was just so little and really not trained to be without a leash and what fun was going to the woods if you had to be on a leash?

Rodney got dropped off about 10:30, just enough time to meet Hector's mom and Ranger and get their lunches packed up. Rodney was a little nervous about Ruby, but Hector reassured him that Ruby was cool. Rodney was mostly nervous because she was a girl. He liked girls but was pretty shy around them.

Off they went to meet up with Ruby, she could see them coming as she walked towards them and started waving. Ranger ran up to greet her first and Ruby knelt down to give him a proper return greeting.

All the way to the edge of the woods Hector talked about the woods and all the things they discovered there this past summer. He was excited, Ruby never seen him this excited. He found a best friend, thought Ruby with a smile on her heart. First, they stopped at the edge of the pond, all three had their boots on so they could get really close. They could see little fish swimming all around, "We shoulda brought some fishin' poles!" Rodney exclaimed. Ruby just looked at Hector to see what he would say to that.

"Eh...fishin' ain't all that fun Rodney, there's lots of other things to do here, like this," and he picked up some flat rocks and skimmed them across the top of the water. It took him a while to learn that and he wanted to show Rodney how good at it he was.

They decided to take a little hike through the woods before unpacking their lunches. As they walked, they tried to scrunch in the dried leaves and reach for the low ones on the trees. Ruby and Rodney were getting along good and Hector was happy for that. He hoped for one good friend in his new house and now he had two! Suddenly up ahead Rodney noticed something that looked like a cave made out of leaves and branches. He started towards it shouting for the others to follow him. Hector knew that was not a good idea to get into that, but it was too late,

Rodney was on his hands and knees crawling through the cave-like opening. Hector went to the opening and looked in. Rodney was pretty far in. Hector knew this wasn't going to end well.

"Um, Rodney? You might want to come out of there…… It's poison ivy."

"What??? Are you kidding me right now?" and he backed out in record time. When he stood up, there were leaves in his hair. He started to brush himself off.

"We better head back to my house," Hector said, "My mom will know what to do."

So, the three of them hiked back out of the woods towards Hector's house. Hector and Ruby were walking with a space between them and Rodney for fear of it getting on them.

By the time they got back to Hector's house, Rodney was itching pretty badly and his eyes were swelling up. It looked like it was hard for him to keep open the little slits that were left.

"Oh my goodness," exclaimed Hector's mom, "What happened?"

They told her what happened and she went right to work on him. She took him to the basement and told him to take all his clothes off and get in a cool shower. Hector would bring him some clean clothes. Then they all left him to take care of himself. Hector's mom called Rodney's mom and told her what happened. When Rodney came upstairs with Hector's clothes on Hector and Ruby looked very concerned. His eyes were so puffy and red. He had red blotches on his cheeks and on his hands and neck. They knew better than to crawl through vines and leaves like that in the woods, and just assumed that Rodney would know the rules of the woods, but he didn't.

Rodney was still itching. He kept apologizing to Hector and Ruby for ruining the day. They didn't even think that for a minute and told him so. His mom came then and Hector's mom handed her the plastic bag full of his clothes and shoes. He would go home barefoot. His mom decided to take him to the Dr. because his eyes were so swollen. The Dr. could give him some medication for the itching and to help get his eyes back to normal. He apologized again before he left and Hector told him not to worry about it and to call him later.

Ruby and Hector were speechless. His mom brought their lunches to the table and they ate in silence. Neither knew what to say about what happened. Finally, Hector's mom started a conversation about how to treat poison ivy and how long it would take for him to be back to normal.

"You mean he will have to go to school like that?" Hector asked.

"Yes, it could take a few weeks to go away. Hopefully the swelling will go down in his eyes sooner. It's not your fault that it happened. He's not used to going into the woods and I think he probably ran ahead of you or for some reason you didn't see him going into the ivy patch, right?"

"Yes," said Hector, "He ran ahead because he thought it looked like a cave. I think he wanted to explore it. We were having so much fun! I can't believe he will have to go to school like that, I feel sorry for him."

Ruby thought about that too, going to school looking like a ripe strawberry. Ryan would probably be all over him for this. Maybe his mom would let him stay home from school for a few days. She hoped so for his sake.

Chapter Thirty-Two

Ryan did not have a very good weekend. He thought a lot about Ruby, Hector, and Rodney and wondered what they were doing. His parents fought and his father drank all weekend as usual, but at least they left him alone instead of dragging him into their fights. He was so tired of it; he just wanted a life like other kids had. No one invited him anywhere and of course he didn't invite anyone over because he never knew what was going to be going on. He played his video games and just hung out in his room. He did have a bike and he went out a little bit for a ride, but he was just so bored, and lonely. Having lunch with Rodney and Hector seemed to make him lonelier. Lonely for a real friend.

Back at school on Monday morning, Ryan wasn't sure how he wanted to act anymore. He felt mostly confused and sad. Hector noticed on the bus he sat by himself and didn't say anything rude or obnoxious to anyone. Hector was nervous for Rodney. His eyes were still a bit swollen and he had rashes on his face and hands. Ryan must not have noticed yet. Ryan and Rodney got to their locker and into homeroom without any problems. It was as if no one noticed Rodney at all, and this was the perfect chance for anybody to make fun of him. They both wondered what was going on. Ryan was really quiet and keeping to himself. Lunch time was coming up and still nothing from Ryan. Hector and Rodney wondered out loud to each other, but neither could figure Ryan out lately. It's one thing to be bullied on a daily basis all day long, but when it stops abruptly it's kinda scary.

Ryan thought maybe Mrs. Grace could help him figure this out, but they no longer had lunch alone. He would have to ask for time to see her on his own and he didn't know if he could do that because what would he say to her? How could she help him? No, that's not a good idea, thought Ryan as he headed to the lunch room to get his tray of food. He wished he could do this for breakfast too.

Hector and Rodney grabbed their lunches from their locker and headed to Mrs. Grace's office. Lunch was always interesting lately. They never knew what Mrs. Grace would want to bring up. It was a little uncomfortable, but for some reason they both looked forward to it.

Rodney kept his head down, so Mrs. Grace would not see his face.

"Hello, hello...go right in boys!" Mrs. Grace was coming up behind them, she sure seemed to be in a good mood today. Ryan and Rodney said nothing as they walked in. "Did you boys hear me out there in the hall?" Mrs. Grace asked. They both nodded their heads. "I can't hear your heads nodding, can you speak up and say hello back when someone greets you?"

"Hello Mrs. Grace," they both said with no enthusiasm. They put their lunches down on the table and took a seat. Ryan came in with his tray and didn't say anything to anyone, didn't even look at anyone. Oh boy, thought Hector, what's this lunch going to be like, he looks miserable.

Once they were all seated, Mrs. Grace started the conversation off with asking how their weekend was. Ryan snickered with his head down shoveling in his food. He hoped she wouldn't ask him to share what his weekend was like, but he sure wanted to know what happened to Rodney's face.

"Rodney? Why don't start us off and share with us what you did this weekend," Rodney kept his head down and didn't say anything. "Rodney? Can you look at me?" Mrs. Grace could see he was purposely keeping his head down today. She thought they had made some progress last week but maybe not. He looked up and right at her. "Oh Rodney! What happened to your face...and your neck and hands?" she exclaimed. Ryan waited patiently to find out what he had been wondering all day. Hector sat quietly, he felt so bad for his friend.

Rodney could feel Ryan staring at him. It felt like he was laughing at him, but actually Ryan just sat and waited for the explanation. Very slowly Rodney started out, "I went into the woods with Hector and Ruby, I saw what looked like a tunnel or cave made up of leaves and sticks. I crawled into it. It was poison ivy." He put his head back down. He felt like crying but he didn't. He was so embarrassed as he waited for Ryan's laugh or remarks, but Ryan just stared at him with his mouth open.

"That is so cool," said Ryan. "It looks like you're wearing a mask, does it hurt?" he asked. He was so intrigued. He wasn't mocking him; he was actually impressed.

"No," said Rodney, "it itches and it's gross." He put his head back down and hoped that Mrs. Grace would move on to Hector or Ryan.

"Oh Rodney, I'm sorry that happened to you, but were you having fun before this happened?" she asked.

"Yes," said Rodney, "a lot of fun, it's a really cool place to explore and there's a small pond we skipped rocks in. We saw deer, and bunnies too." Suddenly he realized he was talking and excited about it so he stopped.

"How fun," Mrs. Grace said, "who did you go with?"

"I went with Hector and Ruby; the woods are behind their houses."

Ryan was silently taking it all in. He felt jealous and started to feel that anger coming back, like he wanted to hurt them.

"Ryan, did you have a good weekend? Why don't you tell us what you did?"

Ugh, thought Ryan. "I don't want to talk about it," he said. Who wants to hear that he hung out in his room while his parents fought and drank all weekend? He wished he could just slink down under the table and disappear. "This whole lunch thing is lame," he said, "who cares if he got poison ivy and had fun, who really wants to hear about it?" His voice was raised a little bit and Mrs. Grace let him know that that was unacceptable. He just rolled his eyes. Hector and Rodney felt like it was about time the real Ryan came out. He was back to his own self again just in time for the bell to ring and get them back to class.

Mrs. Grace excused Hector and Rodney but asked Ryan to stay for a moment. Ryan thought he was going to be in trouble again, maybe more detention. Hector and Rodney felt relieved that he would stay there, it would give them a chance to go to their locker and get into class before Ryan could do anything to them.

"Ryan, I notice that you are struggling with the other boys having fun on their weekend. Can you tell me what you did?" Mrs. Grace asked after Hector and Rodney left.

"Why do you want to know anyways, Mrs. Grace?" Ryan sneered. "Who really cares?"

"I do Ryan, I care. Let's sit down and talk about this." She invited him back to the table and he sat down.

Ryan was resistant but he did tell her about his home life. Then she understood his behavior a little more. This kid was isolated in a world of chaos in his own home. She talked to him about alcoholism and told him that it wasn't his fault that his father drank or that his parents fought all the time. She told him there was a group of kids that went to a program called Alateen. It was right after school, in the church across the street and he could get the late bus after the meeting.

"I ain't goin' to no church," he said with much pain in his voice. He wanted some help so bad but *church*? He thought.

"It's in a church but not run by the church, they just rent the space for their meetings. I think you would like it. There are other kids there that have similar home lives and they help each other by sharing with each other. I wish you would give it a try Ryan. Just go a few times and then decide whether or not you want to keep going. I think there's a meeting today after school, if you want to call home and let your mom know that you will be late, you can use the phone."

"Like they really care that I even come home! I don't need no church thing, just leave me alone!" He got up and stormed out of the office.

Well, thought Mrs. Grace, that didn't go too well. But she knew that she would not give up on him. She let him go to his class and decided she would call him back down during his study hall later in the day. Let him think about it for a little while. She hoped he wouldn't take it out on any of the other kids in his class, or the teacher.

He whipped open the door to the classroom and walked in late. The teacher stopped teaching and looked over at Ryan. Hector never saw him look so mean. "Looks like you are late to class Ryan, do you have a pass?"

Ryan debated whether to answer or not. "Go ask Mrs. Grace for a pass if you want one," sneered Ryan as he walked over to his seat.

"I'm sorry Ryan but I can't let you stay in class unless you go get a pass from Mrs. Grace. I'm sure if you were there with her, she will have no problem giving you a pass. Go on now."

Ryan almost knocked the desk over when he got up. He stormed out of the classroom. When he got out in the hall, he wasn't sure what to do, but he knew he was not going back to Mrs. Grace, so he left the school. Once he got outside, he had to decide what to do with the rest of his day. He seen that stupid church across the street that Mrs. Grace was talking about, he'd never go in there, he thought. But he couldn't go home that was for sure. So, he just started walking. On the way towards home he came upon a park so he went in. There was a gym set with swings so he took a seat on the swing and just started to swing, harder and harder he pumped. Higher and higher he went. It felt good to use some of the anger energy he had built up. Suddenly he heard a voice asking if he was Ryan Jackson.

"Who wants to know?" he said sarcastically. It was a police officer, *oh great*, Ryan thought.

"I'm here to take you back to school, either that or I can take you to the station and call your parents."

Ryan slowed the swing to a stop. He just sat there for a few minutes thinking. He knew if his parents were called, he would get a beating when he got home. But go back to school? Why couldn't everyone just leave him alone? He went with the police officer back to school, into Mrs. Grace's office. He slunk into the chair and waited for the big lecture and more detention. He didn't even care anymore. Let them do whatever they wanted.

"Ryan, good to see you back," she said with a smile on her face. Why was she always so happy? It was irritating.

"Did I have a choice?" he said.

"Yes," she said, "you do. Would you rather have the police officer take you home?" She knew he did not want that. "Here's the plan, Ryan, I'm not going to give you punishment for today. I know you are upset about the idea of going to the Alateen program after school, but I think it will really help you. I'm going to give you some pamphlets and you can take them home with you and read them over. It might help you make the decision to go. What could it hurt if you tried it out? It's free and it would delay the time you have to go home."

"Ok, ok...I'll take the pamphlets, but I still don't want to go to no church."

"I told you, you would not be going to a church service and no one from the church will approach you, it's only about the Alateen program."

"It's today?" Ryan asked.

"Yes, right after school. It lasts for an hour and then you could catch the bus home after that."

"OK, I'll go...but I'm probably not going to like it!"

Mrs. Grace felt relieved. She gave him the pamphlets anyways and told him to keep them and read them all. She gave him a pass to go back to class but before she let him go, she told him to sit down and take some deep breaths, calm himself down a little bit. She didn't want him to go back and take out his anger on whoever was in his path.

Ryan felt like his insides were ripping apart. He was so riled up, and he didn't seem to know a real reason why. She suggested Alateen, big deal, why did it bother him so much. He had such a stomach ache and a head ache too. What kind of kids were going to be at this Alateen meeting? Would some of them know him from school? Whose business was it anyways?

The rest of the day was uneventful for Rodney and Hector. They didn't know what was happening but it seemed to be going their way. Ryan wasn't even on the bus going home that day and so that was a plus for them. They talked to Ruby on the way home. Rodney really wanted another chance at going to the woods. He thought they would say no way, but they both agreed that they go again before the snow came.

Chapter Thirty-Three

Ryan was feeling really nervous about this Alateen thing. Why did he agree to this, why didn't he just go home and take his beating like normal? After he got his things out of his locker he headed out across the street to the church. He thought he'd just hang out outside to see what kind of kids went inside. He waited and waited. A few kids went in but they all looked normal so he didn't think they were going to Alateen. He finally decided to go in, but he wasn't going to talk.

Ryan walked into the church and followed the signs to the basement of the church. Well at least it wasn't in the church part, he thought. There were about 10 kids in there and 2 adults. One of the adults came over to welcome him. Some of the kids looked a little familiar but he didn't know their names. He sat at the table and the adult introduced him as a newcomer. Each kid around the table said "Hi Ryan, we're glad you're here." He just sat there and didn't say anything, it just felt so weird and he was unsure of how to act, everyone was so friendly. They started the meeting with the 12 Steps of

Alcoholics Anonymous. Everyone took turns reading, including him. Then they decided to do a meeting where everyone shared why they came and why they keep coming back. They said he didn't have to share if he didn't want to so he sat back to listen. It was weird though because as each person took their turn, they weren't afraid to tell things that were a secret in his house. It made him feel more relaxed as each person shared. He might like it here even though it made him feel a little afraid for his turn to share.

When the hour was up, Ryan went back over to the bus loop to catch the late bus. There were a few other kids there but he didn't know any of them. He heard snickers behind him and suddenly he was shoved almost into the street. It was no accident. He turned around and some bigger kids were standing there laughing. His good relaxed feeling left him in an instant. He was angry and was ready to strike back with some comment that he couldn't think of off the top of his head, but he wasn't going to run away, or slink away like a coward. Just then the bus came and he boarded. He sat in the front near the bus driver. When the bigger kids got on, each one smacked him in the head as they went past. He shrunk into his seat. He felt humiliated and angry. What could he do? They were bigger than him. He could hear them in the back of the bus making comments about the little 6th grader in the front of the bus. He wished he would have walked home, it's pretty far but it would be better than this. At first it didn't even occur to him that he did the same thing to Rodney and Hector. Somehow, he rationalized it in his mind that it was different, even though he was starting to feel different towards them both. He was so confused.

When Ryan got home it was really quiet and he wondered what was going on. Usually his dad would be sitting at the kitchen table drinking his beer and mom would be somewhere in the house doing some housework or she would be in the kitchen trying to start a fight with him. He looked around for a note or something that would tell him where they were. He wasn't afraid to be home alone but it was not something that happened often. He decided to find something to eat, make himself some dinner. He searched the cupboards and the refrigerator. Not much here, but he did come up with some mac and cheese, so he fixed that for himself and sat down in front of the TV. It was a few hours before his mom came home, without his dad. When his mom came into the living room, he could tell she had been crying. Her face was all red and blotchy. She had Kleenex in her hand and was wiping her nose. It wasn't that she had been crying, she was still crying. *Oh no*, he thought, *something musta happened to my dad*. "Mom, what's wrong?" asked Ryan. She sat down next to him on the couch. He didn't know how she was going to talk since she was crying so hard, but she calmed herself down long enough to tell Ryan that his dad was in jail.

"JAIL???" Ryan was in shock. He didn't know how to respond. He sat and waited for her to tell him the details, but she just sat and cried.

"Why, mom? Why is he in jail? What did he do? Can you get him out?" He had so many questions and she just kept crying.

Once she was able to calm herself down enough to talk to Ryan, she told him that his dad was caught driving while he was drunk. He went out to the store to get more beer and went through a stop sign so a police officer pulled him over. His mom thought it was all her fault because he wanted her to go out to the store, and she refused and then they had a fight and he left very angry. One of the kids at his Alateen meeting had a dad that went to jail too. He talked about it to the group and Ryan remembered thinking, *at least my dad never had to go to jail.* He even thought maybe he didn't belong there because of that. Suddenly he looked forward to going back to that meeting to hear more. His mom started making phone calls to try and get some money to bail him out. At first Ryan was upset about his father being in jail, but then thought about how quiet it would be without him here. Then he felt guilty for thinking about wanting him to stay in jail. Ryan's day of confusion was just getting worse. He went to his room to try and do his homework, let his mom figure this out for herself. For all his troubles, he did do well in school. He kept up on his homework assignments and finished any projects assigned in school. Most of it bored him, but he always handed in his homework. Ryan's father spent the night in jail. Ryan went to bed with a stomach ache and a lot of anxiety. He couldn't stop thinking about it and thinking about the boy at the Alateen meeting, wondering how he seemed to be ok. Ryan wasn't sure he could share anything without anger or tears and he sure didn't want to cry in front of all those kids.

Chapter Thirty-Four

The next day at Lunch Bunch, Mrs. Grace brought up the homework she gave them a few days ago. All three kids just froze and looked at her like they didn't know what she was talking about. She thought this might happen, so she explained the homework again and just decided to have them come up with questions right then. Ryan was half way done with his lunch and she turned to him and asked him to go first. He had no desire to do any of this. It became lame again. He remained quiet and Mrs. Grace asked him again to come up with a question for Hector or Rodney.

"I don't have a question for either of these lame losers! I'm outta here now!" He pushed back and his chair fell backwards with a crash. He stormed out of the room and out of school. Hector and Rodney didn't know what to think. They thought Ryan was starting to get a little better, treating them better, but just now showed them different. Back to the old Ryan. Again.

Mrs. Grace went after him, but he was too fast. He was out the door before she even got out to the hallway. She had to call the principal who called the police again. Ryan ran and ran. He didn't know where he was going, but he just wanted to be far away. The park was up ahead so he ran there. No one was around and he was glad of that because he was crying and could not stop. Suddenly he saw the police car, he hid in the bushes, but the officer had already seen him. As the officer got closer, Ryan felt such fear of being found. He didn't want to go back to school, or go home. He didn't know what he wanted or who could help him. The officer had to chase him down but he caught him and put him in the back of the police car. *Now, I'm just like my dad*, thought Ryan. He wiped away his tears and tried to toughen up, but he felt like he was breaking apart from the inside out.

"I'm taking you back to school young man, I'm sure they will call your parents from there. You have to go to school."

"Whatever," said Ryan. He no longer cared. He was trying hard to feel nothing, not even fear. If his dad was still in jail, then he would get no beating when he got home. His mom would be easier on him, she would probably just start crying again.

When the police officer brought Ryan back into school, he took him straight to Mrs. Grace's office. Her and the principal were there waiting for him.

"Have a seat, Ryan," Mr. Scott said. "We need to find out what's going on with you. I called your mother and she told me a little bit of what's going on at your house. It's a lot to handle and we want you to know that we are here for you." Mr. Scott was more concerned for Ryan than angry at him.

"Whatever," Ryan slumped down into the chair and just hung his head, he didn't believe him. He felt lost and alone. He wondered in his mind if anyone cared about him. He wished they would all leave him alone, but he also wished someone would care about him. He was hurting so much that that was all he could focus on; he just did not know what to do next.

Mr. Scott and Mrs. Grace talked to Ryan for a long time in Mrs. Grace's office. Ryan started to relax a little bit and listen to them, but he still didn't trust them so he didn't share much. Mrs. Grace told him that it wasn't his fault that his father drank so much or that he drove while drinking either. She told him that he didn't have to be ashamed of him either.

"Did you go to the Alateen meeting Ryan," Mrs. Grace asked.

"Yes," he said. She wanted to know what he thought about the meeting. She just wanted to get him talking but he was just responding with short one-word answers. They kept encouraging him and soon he started to respond a little more as they gained his trust. Sometimes when bad things happen in a home it becomes like a secret surrounded by shame and embarrassment. It's hard to break it. As he was talking about his father, Ryan started to cry and then he was really embarrassed. He just didn't know how to act, he never had anyone really want to hear what he was thinking about or even want to know about him.

Ryan told them about the Alateen meeting and how everyone said hello to him and told him they hoped he came back. He told them about all the kids sharing one at a time about why they came to Alateen and how it helped them. It seemed like once he started talking, he couldn't stop and they were listening to him.

Mrs. Grace and Mr. Scott kept reinforcing the idea that his parent's behavior was not his responsibility and anything that they did was not his fault and that he could not control it or them. Ryan could not change them, but he could change how he reacted. He didn't have to beat up on others or bully them. It wouldn't make him feel any better. Ryan was starting to feel a little better, but he dreaded going home. Was his father going to be there or would it just be his crying mother. He still felt confused, but now he had some support and he trusted them. He had some hope that he would be ok whether his parents shaped up or not.

The day was almost over and Ryan missed most of his classes. Mrs. Grace assured him that his teachers would give him the work to do at home. He was so tired out from all the emotion during this day, but he knew he would get his homework done. He always made that a priority, he wasn't sure why but it felt important to him. Just as he was about to go back to class, his mom arrived. She was really nervous but at least she wasn't crying. Mrs. Grace gave him a pass to go back to class and told him she would talk to his mom. He was a little scared about that, but then he remembered that he was trusting in Mrs. Grace. She seemed to care about him, he wasn't sure why but it felt kinda good.

Mrs. Grace talked to Ryan's mom for a while. She told her about the Alateen group Ryan had went to and also told her of a group for her called Al-Anon. She gave her a schedule of meetings and hoped she would try it out. They talked about alcoholism for a little while. Ryan's mom left feeling a little bit better; thinking she would try out this Al-Anon. Why not?

Ryan got back to class and walked in quietly, gave his pass to the teacher and found his seat. He felt strangely calm. What a day! He looked around at all the kids in his class. He decided right then that his bullying would stop. When he looked at Rodney and Hector, he felt a longing to be friends with them, but he didn't know how to go about it. I'll talk to Mrs. Grace about that, he thought.

The bus ride home was rather quiet. Ryan sat behind Hector and Rodney. He didn't try to talk to them or anyone else. He just sat quietly and when it was his turn, he got off the bus without a word to anyone. He still dreaded going in the house but remembered what Mrs. Grace and Mr. Scott had said about not being responsible for his parent's behavior. His mom met him at the door, dad was still in jail. She could not come up with the money to bail him out. Ryan felt relieved. His mom was still a little jittery, but she seemed relieved that he was out of the house for a few days too. She had to work in the evening but Ryan didn't mind, he had homework to keep him busy, and his thoughts too. He found himself looking forward to next week when he could go back to Alateen.

Chapter Thirty-Five

Ryan spent a quiet night at home doing homework, watching TV and playing a little Mine Craft. He felt so empty and tired. He never felt lonelier, he found himself wishing he had some friends like Hector and Rodney that he could call and hang out with. When his mom came home from work, they sat on the couch and talked about what was happening in their home. His mom was at a loss about what to do. Ryan told her about his Alateen meeting and she told him she decided to go to an Al-Anon meeting the next day. He felt a little hope, like things might be able to get better, but he worried that his dad would be mad when he found out they were going. His mom was a little worried about that too. She didn't say it but Ryan could tell she was nervous when she talked about it. His dad would be home the next day. Ryan felt a little guilty because he felt so much better with him gone. He was afraid to tell his mom that, but he thought she was feeling the same way.

When Ryan got on the bus the next day, he was very quiet again. He sat behind Hector and Rodney. His friends at the back of the bus didn't know what to do with themselves, so they just fooled around amongst themselves. When the bus arrived at the school, Ryan got off and went straight to Mrs. Grace's office. He felt like a mess on the inside and wasn't sure how he wanted to act.

"Good morning, Ryan! What brings you to my office this morning?"

Ryan told her he didn't know, so she invited him to have a seat and tell her about it. He told her that he felt confused on how to act. He didn't want to be mean anymore, but what about his friends that expected him to "lead the way," how would he act towards them? How do you just change the way you are?

Mrs. Grace felt so relieved for Ryan. She knew it wasn't going to be an overnight occurrence, but Ryan was ready to change and she was happy for him.

"First you have to recognize that you want to change, and it sounds like you have done that. Next you have to show that on the outside. You are changing rapidly on the inside and now you have to show it. You can start with Hector and Rodney. You have time to practice at lunch time, just getting to know them. Let them build their trust towards you. Keep going to your Alateen meetings and just learn about who you really are. You'll be ok, Ryan. It might be a little rough for a while with your "friends," They won't understand, but you will be setting an example for them. Hopefully they will follow your example and stop the bullying in class and in the halls. It can be a very confusing transition and if you ever need to talk with someone about what you are feeling, please don't hesitate to come to me. I will always have time for you."

Ryan put his head down. He didn't know what to say, he was near tears. Finally, someone would listen to him and hear him. He hoped his mom would find the help she needed too. She said she was going to go to the Al-Anon meetings and he hoped she did. He planned on and looked forward to going to his Alateen meetings and making some real friends. In the back of his mind he worried about what it would be like when he went home today. His dad would be there. Would things go right back to how they were or would his dad be nicer since he went to jail? All he knew was that today was his Alateen meeting and he was looking forward to it. He decided not to take that late bus home anymore. He wanted to avoid those bigger kids so he would walk home even though it was a little far it would give him time to think about what he would hear at his meeting. He actually had things to look forward to now and that made him feel good.

That day at Lunch Bunch Ryan had a question for Hector. He wanted to know how he learned how to solve the Rubik's Cube and if he would show him how he did it. He shyly asked Hector at lunch. Hector was cautious, he didn't trust Ryan. He'd seen him go back to his old self many times and he was afraid Ryan would make fun of him somehow over this. He answered him though.

"I learned it by watching YouTube videos," he said without looking up.

Ryan thought about that for a few minutes. *So, he taught himself*, thought Ryan...hmmm, I wonder if I could do that too. He thought he would go a little further and asked, "Would you bring yours in and show me how you solve it?"

Hector was a little surprised. He still did not trust Ryan and it would take a while to get there, but what harm would there be in bringing his Rubik's Cube to lunch, he told Ryan he would bring it the next day. Rodney just sat and listened to what was happening. Could Ryan be changing for good now? He wasn't sure he trusted him either. Mrs. Grace was pleased and she told them so.

Ryan shared that day in Alateen. He shared about his dad going to jail and how he felt guilty for not wanting him to come home, but that he would probably be there when he got home. He was nervous and had a stomach ache just thinking about it. It seemed like things were just starting to get better, his mom was not crying as much and now his dad was coming home. Would he ruin everything like usual? After the meeting one of the other boys came up to him and started sharing his experience with his own dad coming home from jail. He told him he had similar feelings. That made Ryan feel better to know that he was not the only one with the feelings he was having. The two boys exchanged phone numbers and promised to call each other. Ryan walked home feeling much better. He even had a smile on his face at the thought of having a friend, a real one! Should he call him tonight? It took him about 45 minutes to walk home.

Ryan was glad to have walked home. It gave him time to think about what was happening in his life and how he wanted to change and also about what it was going to be like when he got home. When he walked into the kitchen, his dad was not at the table drinking. That's a good sign he thought. He was in the living room watching

TV, with a beer in his hand. Ryan's heart sank. He thought for sure that the stay in jail would stop his dad's drinking. His mom was not around, she already left for work. Ryan walked into the living room and just stood in the doorway. His dad looked at him and set his beer down. He asked him to come sit down next to him, he wanted to talk to him about what happened. Ryan was a little scared. He was still drinking beer which meant that whatever he said or did, didn't mean much. He had promised things before while still drinking and those promises were broken sometimes within minutes. Ryan sat down and waited for his dad to speak.

"Ryan, I wanted to tell you that I'm sorry that I got arrested and put in jail. I promise it will never happen again."

Ryan did not believe him, but he just nodded his head. He already knew not to speak up to his dad. It never did any good. He asked to be excused so that he could go do his homework. His dad reminded him that he would have to make dinner for them. It was just warming up what his mom left for them, and setting the table, but Ryan hoped that his dad would take over that chore. His dad seemed calmer but it didn't look like much had changed. He was sure it was just a matter of time before the yelling and hitting would start up again.

Ryan fixed dinner and set the table. They ate in silence and then Ryan cleaned up the kitchen and put the dishes in the dishwasher. His dad went back to the couch to continue watching TV, so Ryan took the phone and went to his room to do homework. Once he got to his room, he thought about calling his new friend. He was nervous to do that in case his friend was not home or did not want to hear from him, so he didn't. He just started right in on his homework. After a while the phone rang. He answered it right away. To his surprise it was his new friend! He called to see how things went when he got home. They talked for a little while and Ryan felt really good about the phone call. Things were looking up! He just might get some new friends that were real! He went to bed that night feeling peaceful in his heart.

Chapter Thirty-Six

Hector was trying to decide which Rubik Cube to take with him to school the next day. Maybe Ryan would just forget about it or act like he didn't really care about it. He had a lot of Rubik's Cubes so he decided to take a few with him in the little bag he had to hold them all. School was going a little better these days. Having lunch with Ryan and Rodney wasn't as bad as he thought it would be. He actually kind of enjoyed it and sometimes even looked forward to it as long as Ryan was in a good mood. He still did not trust him though and it felt like he was waiting for something to happen again. It seemed like every time he started to be ok with Ryan and Ryan ok with him, something would happen and they'd be back to the beginning again, getting made fun of and bullied. Hector made his Rubik's choices and started on his homework. Rodney called and they talked a little bit about Hector bringing the Rubik's Cube to lunch. Rodney didn't trust Ryan either, he hoped it would all work out.

Ruby was doing her homework when her mom popped her head in the doorway to let her know she had a phone call. From Andrea. Ruby just stared at the phone in her mom's hand. What could Andrea want?

"Hello?" Ruby quietly said into the phone.

"Hi Ruby, its Andrea. I just wanted to call and say hello and see how you are liking school."

Ruby didn't know how to respond so she was silent.

"Are you there, Ruby?"

"Yes," said Ruby, "I just wonder why you are really calling me."

"Look, I was just calling to say hi. Maybe I shouldn't have called," she said sarcastically.

"No," Ruby said, "its ok...I'm doing good. I like middle school, do you?"

"Ruby?" Andrea said.

"Yes Andrea, I'm here, are you ok?

"I just wanted to tell you I'm sorry. I miss being your friend. I guess it's ok if you want to be friends with losers."

Ruby's hope fell. She thought Andrea was going to apologize for the way she behaved. She wasn't sure how to respond so she was quiet and just waited for what Andrea would say next.

Finally, when Andrea didn't say anything, Ruby said, "Hector and Rodney are not losers, they are my friends. If anyone said anything nasty about you, I would stick up for you too. If you would give them a chance, you could be their friend too. They are fun to be with. We've been going to the woods and just getting together to hang out since school started. They are cool and I like them both. So, if you're going to still call them losers, then I don't think our friendship will last."

Andrea was silent. She thought for sure Ruby would have gotten over those two losers by now and want her friendship back, but here was Ruby sticking up for them. What was it about them that she liked? Maybe she should give it another try. She'd have to think about it.

"Well, I have to go now," said Andrea. "I just wanted to say hi, so good bye."

"Ok," said Ruby, "see you around."

They both hung up. Ruby felt stunned. She took the phone back out to the living room and talked to her mom about the phone call. Her mom was proud of her for sticking up for her new friends. "Don't back down, Ruby, you're doing the right thing. You are a fine example for others."

Ruby still didn't know what to think about Andrea's phone call, she felt unsettled, but she went back to her homework. Maybe Andrea was coming around, who knew? She finished up her homework and decided to take Bonnet out for a little walk. Maybe the fresh air would clear her head.

She went out the front door and started walking towards Hector's house. Hector must have had the same idea at the same time, because here he came towards her with Ranger. The two dogs were glad to see each other and Ruby told Hector about her phone call. Hector had no advice for her, he just listened and said "hmmm." They let the subject go and started talking about when they could get together and hang out or go to the woods.

Chapter Thirty-Seven

Ryan couldn't wait for lunch today. He was sure he could learn the Rubik's Cube. Hector was also looking forward to lunch today. He hoped Ryan would not back down and start being nasty again. All three boys were feeling hopeful as they walked into Mrs. Grace's office. They all sat down and Hector wasn't sure if he should bring out his Cubes right away or wait until they were done eating lunch, so he waited. They all ate quickly and Mrs. Grace could sense a big change in the boys, she was happy for them. After lunch Hector brought out his easiest Cube first. He had Hector mix it all up for him and then he solved it. Ryan was very impressed and wanted to learn it. He thought it was so cool. Hector started to teach him when the bell rang. Hector promised to bring it the next day. For the first time they all walked back to class together. Mrs. Grace's smile was big. It was working! They were becoming friends.

The rest of the day was uneventful for Hector and Rodney. Ryan really seemed to have changed this time. His friends were a little quieter in the back of the room lately and it seemed like Ryan was separating himself from them. On the bus, Ryan always sat behind Rodney and Hector now. He didn't talk to them, but he didn't bully them either.

Ruby, Hector and Rodney got together at Ruby's that evening after homework. They started talking about Ryan and the possibility of asking him to join them in an afternoon in the woods. All three were still a little leery, but decided to go ahead and ask him. They didn't know why they should after all that he'd done to them, but they liked him for some reason.

Hector brought his Rubik's Cubes with him to lunch every day that week. He taught Ryan about algorithms and encouraged him to look at YouTube videos to learn more. By the end of the week, Ryan was starting to get it. He was still working on the easiest one, but he was starting to understand it. He now was nicer to them in class and didn't shove them in the hallways. Things were definitely changing.

On Friday at lunch Hector asked Ryan if he wanted to get together with them on Saturday and hike into the woods. Ryan just stared at him like he didn't hear him. In his mind he was just so shocked, he didn't know how to respond. He wanted to go of course, but what would it be like? Having lunch with them and Mrs. Grace at school in this little office was one thing, but spending the day with them with no one there to make sure everything was going ok? He had some fear but he also had some excitement. Friends! Friends to hang out with! Isn't this what he wanted? Now that the opportunity was there, he was afraid of it.

Mrs. Grace sat waiting for an answer too. Finally, she said to Ryan, "Ryan, Hector just asked you a question, aren't you going to answer him?" You can see how they depended on Mrs. Grace to intervene to make things go smoother. She would not be there in the woods with them.

Ryan took a few more moments to freak out in his mind and then he said, "Sure," like it was a normal thing. He wanted more than anything to say "YES!" but he still wanted to appear cool. So, it was set. He would ask his mom to drop him off at Hector's on Saturday at noon. He could barely contain his excitement! He would finally find out what they did in these woods and what it would be like to spend a day with friends.

The boys couldn't wait to tell Ruby. They had fear too, but also the excitement. Both boys were glad Ruby would be there too. She always seemed to know the right thing to do. She could be their Mrs. Grace out in the woods! They decided to pack lunches and take them to the woods. Picnic first and then exploring.

Chapter Thirty-Eight

Saturday came and Ryan was up early. He was so nervous about spending the day with Hector and Rodney. He didn't know Ruby that well, but she was a girl! What had he gotten himself into? But the other side of his mind was looking forward to it and even excited for it. His mom already had agreed to take him to Hector's house at noon, they would pack lunches there. Hector's mom liked to bake so Ryan knew there would be cookies involved in the packing. By 11 o'clock, Ryan had such a stomach ache. His mom was trying to calm him down. She knew he didn't have many friends, if any, because he never brought any home and never seemed to be invited anywhere. She didn't think he should be this nervous and was concerned about him. She wasn't sure how to help him. He was so mad at himself because he knew it was just a nervous stomach, why was he so afraid and nervous? Maybe he should cancel, but he really wanted to go!

He wished he could talk to Mrs. Grace. Who else could he talk to about this stomach ache? He didn't want to tell his mom the real reason he was nervous because then he would have to tell her the whole story about how nasty he had been to these two boys. Ryan thought if he talked to anyone they would not understand and think he was a big wuss. Big bad Ryan afraid to have friends! Then a thought came to him, his Alateen friend! Yes, he could call him. He already knew a lot about Ryan so he wouldn't have to go into all the details of his behavior. So, he called him and talked for a little while. His friend told him he understood how he was feeling, that he too had a similar experience when he first started going to Alateen. He didn't have friends for the longest time and was so unsure of what to do with one. But he asked Ryan, what is the worst thing that could happen? He could always call his mom to come get him. He told Ryan to give these new friends a chance, and give himself a chance too. He hoped he would try to relax a little bit and just see what it was like. When Ryan hung up, he felt a little better and decided he would go. For all his mom's trying to help him to calm down, it didn't work and just this phone call to an Alateen friend seemed to have calmed him enough to agree to go.

Soon it was time to go. Ryan was still jittery, but determined to go see what friends do and how they get along. He got in the car and fastened his seatbelt. His mom told him he could call her at any time if he wanted to come home. So off they went to Hector's house so he could "hang with friends." Just a normal thing for a kid his age, right?

When Ryan knocked on the door, he didn't have to wait long. Ranger was there barking and jumping at the door with Hector right behind him. Ryan was not used to dogs and had a little fear, but within minutes he was kneeling down petting him and getting licked by his new friend Ranger. Hector stood and watched this boy who seemed to hate him weeks ago be so gentle and welcoming to his dog. Hector was a little nervous about today too. Him and Rodney had talked about it a little bit, both were nervous. How was this going to work out they wondered, and both were glad Ruby was coming along. Ryan was the first one there. It was a little awkward for both boys. Hector wasn't sure what to do next, so he invited him into the family room and introduced him to his mom. Ruby and Rodney arrived and they all went to the kitchen to pack lunches for their day in the woods. Ryan just followed along and acted like he fit in, but he was very uncomfortable on the inside.

Chapter Thirty-Nine

Once they got into the woods, Ryan felt himself relaxing a bit. They found a spot for their picnic and as they all unpacked their lunches while Ruby chatted on and on about school and what clubs she was going to join. Her chattering helped the boys feel more at ease and not like they had to find something to talk about right away. Then they put away all their picnic stuff and explored the woods around the water's edge. Ryan was enthralled with nature. Never had he been in the woods like this before. It was just trees, birds and flowers and the water, but for some reason it calmed him. Rodney showed Ryan where he came in contact with the poison ivy a few weeks before and they laughed about it. They saw rabbits and the ducks, and even a couple of deer and Ryan started to feel like he fit in. The other boys were feeling good about the outing too, they always loved to be in the woods anyways, but today they felt like they made a new friend. Ryan's mom picked him up in time to have dinner and Ryan chatted his mom's ear off all the way home. She was so happy for her son. Things were looking better for their family.

Ryan's dad decided to go to Alcoholics Anonymous and had not drank in a few days. It was not going to get better overnight, but they definitely were on their way to a better homelife.

When they got to school on Monday, Ryan couldn't wait to tell Mrs. Grace about his weekend. Mrs. Grace was so happy to hear it. She thought the kids were ready to graduate from Lunch Bunch and she told them about it at lunch that day. All three boys just sat there silently. They didn't want to give up Lunch Bunch, they liked having lunch together and talking with Mrs. Grace. Mrs. Grace decided to give them two more weeks of dining together before sending them back to the cafeteria. She mentioned that they could all sit together in the cafeteria, just like in here, but it just wouldn't be the same, they thought. Mrs. Grace knew it was just the beginning of new things happening for these three boys in middle school. She hoped they would remain friends and be an example for others.

When the two weeks were up, the three boys made the decision that they would sit together in the cafeteria. Ruby still sat with her friends, but always stopped by their table or they would stop by hers, just to say hello. The first day the three boys walked into the cafeteria, Ryan's other "friends" started heckling them, making fun of them and trying to get other kids involved. At first Ryan didn't know what to do, he felt pulled between two worlds. Finally, when the heckling didn't stop, he decided to go over and talk to them. As soon as he started walking towards them, they sat down in their seats and became quiet. They did not know what to expect from Ryan. He never physically controlled them, he only used his 'toughness' and words, but sometimes that's all it takes to control another person. It's the fear of what might happen. Rodney and Hector watched closely. Ryan pulled up a chair and sat down with the "friends." He told them about getting to know Rodney and Hector and about the day in the woods. These "friends" didn't know how to respond to this Ryan, so they just sat with their mouths open with no words coming out. Ryan told them they were welcome to come sit with them, but if they decided not to, then he didn't want to hear anymore insults and heckling going on from them. He got up and walked back to his new real friends and sat down. The four boys just sat there in some sort of shock. Not one of them said anything to each other for a few minutes. Then they looked at each other to see what they thought, and all at once they gathered up their lunches and went to join Ryan and his friends. It was an awkward lunch period for sure, but Hector and Rodney were both so happy that their circle of friends was expanding and middle school might not be so bad after all. They both knew that Mrs. Grace would be so happy for them and proud of them all.

Ruby however, was not to get her friendship back with Andrea. Andrea had her own group of friends and did not want to include Ruby in that since Ruby decided to befriend others that didn't measure up to her idea of what a friend should look like. It's too bad, but sometimes it happens where you have to choose how you want to be, what will be comfortable for you and sometimes you lose friends over it. Inside we all have an inner voice that knows what is right, sometimes we ignore it and sometimes we have to be quiet so we can hear it. It's very easy to judge a person by how they look. It takes a person that listens to that inner voice to take a closer look and see that everyone has something to offer. We don't have to like everybody, but when you don't like someone it doesn't mean you have to be mean to them. Just move on to someone else. There are friends for everybody, to be friendless is a very sad and lonely place to be. If you see someone that seems to be pushed off to the side, you might want to walk over and get to know them a little bit, and then decide if you want to be a friend or just an acquaintance. It's all up to you. Friends come in all colors, sizes and shapes. They wear all different kinds of clothes and have different beliefs.

You can't judge a book by its cover. Sometimes books have really pretty colorful covers and other times they are just plain. The plain ones can have really good stories in them but people don't like to pick them up as much. It's too bad, because the pretty ones sometimes can be very boring and dull and the plain ones can be great stories.

People can be the same. You never know what's inside until you give it a chance and get to know them.

So...

Don't judge a book by its cover!

Character Guide

Ruby

Ruby is 12 years old with long straight brown hair that she wears in braided pigtails. She has freckles across her nose and is five foot tall and very thin. She is an only child and her parents are very loving and open to Ruby experiencing life. Her room is filled with books and games and stuffed animals…and girly stuff like jewelry and Chap Stick and hair bows. She loves to dance and is not afraid to just be who she is, she loves adventure and mystery. Ruby wears red high-top sneakers and her clothes are a mixture of matching and unmatching outfits…her mood picks her style for the day and her mom lets her pick her own style. Her favorite color is red. Ruby has the kind of voice where people know she is in the room, but she's not overwhelming. She gets carried away and sometimes talks too fast for others to keep up. Ruby is very popular in school and has a lot of school friends.

Ruby's mom and dad

Very encouraging parents. Ruby and her mom have a really nice relationship and are able to talk about most things.

Hector's mom and dad

Hector's mom and dad struggled financially for a while. When his dad got a new job, they were able to move into a nicer house and Hector was able to get newer clothes instead of always wearing hand me downs or second-hand clothes. Both parents are very encouraging to Hector and concerned about the bullying that he endures at school.

Hector Fleming

Hector is the new neighbor. He is 12 years old and kinda short and a little "big" for his age, if you know what I mean, some may call him fat. Hector has real short curly blond hair that sticks up all over the place. His clothes are kinda messy. He too is an only child and his parents are very loving and encouraging to him, but he is mostly sad. Hector is shy and withdrawn normally. He doesn't have a lot of friends and usually keeps to himself a lot. He did not want to move to a new city and start over with all the bullying that he experienced on a daily basis at his old school. He doesn't do much outside his house. He likes snacks a lot. His best friend is his dog, Ranger. Hector is really good at solving Rubik's Cubes.

Ranger

Ranger is Hectors dog. He is big and brown according to Ruby, and furry.

Bonnet

Bonnet is Ruby's dog. She's a tiny little dog, white and fluffy.

Andrea

Andrea is a slim girl. Her parents both have good jobs so Andrea has all the latest clothes and accessories. Andrea can be a bit snooty. She's popular and likes to be the center of attention. She often makes fun of others and sometimes gets caught by her teacher and punished for it. But that doesn't seem to stop her. Andrea has brothers and sisters, but is the youngest one. She often feels left out or treated like a baby. She thinks she has a lot of friends but a lot of her friends talk behind her back and say nasty things about her. She knows it but pretends not to. Andrea is Ruby's friend. She does not like Hector at all. She lets Ruby know that she doesn't like him, just by his appearance. Andrea does not like dogs either. She is a bully and judges by first appearance.

Ryan

Also known as Loud Mouth Boy. He is the biggest bully. Comes into the story the first day of school. He comes from a troubled home. His father drinks a lot and his mother tries to stop him. There is a lot of fighting in the home. He wears a red baseball cap backwards and looks tough but actually he's very lonely. He has a following of other bully's in training. They are really only his friend because they are afraid of him. Ryan is good at drawing and is very smart, but no one knows this till he gets in trouble for bullying.

Rodney

Rodney was a shy boy from an elementary school in the area. He was scared to go to middle school because he got picked on a lot in his elementary school. He is a slim boy, with dark hair. He had all the "right" clothes on with name labels and expensive to buy, but he was quiet. He played the guitar and was good at it, but was often too shy to play for anyone. He spent a lot of time in his room. His mom couldn't understand why he didn't invite friends over. He never got invited anywhere either. What she didn't know was that Rodney got bullied on a daily basis. He dreaded going to school every day. He'd get pushed and mocked, ignored and left out. But he didn't tell his parents because he was so ashamed. Rodney didn't know what was wrong with him, why nobody seemed to like him. He was very smart too, and some boys wanted to copy his answers for homework and tests. Even the girls made fun of him, especially at lunch.

Mrs. Mayberry

Mrs. Mayberry is Ruby's homeroom teacher. The first teacher she meets in middle school. She sets down simple rules of homeroom and expects the students to follow through.

Mr. Fink

Mr. Fink is Hector's homeroom teacher. He is a no-nonsense kind of teacher, which works out for Hector.

Mr. Scott

Mr. Scott is the principal. He made sure he knew about the new middle schoolers that were coming into his school. He cares about the kids and does what he can to get to the bottom of things. He treats the students very fairly.

Mrs. Grace

Mrs. Grace is the school counselor. She is very caring and very strict. She believes that all kids deserve a chance. She loves her job and the kids.

Back Cover

<u>Don't Judge a Book by Its Cover!</u> is a book for all ages but geared towards middle schoolers.

Ruby dreams of a new friend when the house next door goes up for sale. When a boy moves in and looks kind of sloppy, and stutters she wonders if he can be a friend. Over the summer she gets to know him and decides he is a very good friend, until she introduces him to one of her best friends and she does not approve of him. Ruby has to decide what kind of person she wants to be and who she wants to be friends with, and it's a struggle. In school her new friend gets bullied and Ruby has to make choices about how she wants to respond.

Join Ruby, Hector, Rodney and Ryan for a year of discoveries about themselves and each other and remember...**Don't Judge a Book by Its Cover!**

About the Author

Susan Potter, also known as Simply Sue, is a mother, a grandmother, a sister, a cousin and a friend. She lives in Tonawanda, NY, which is tucked in between Buffalo and Niagara Falls. Don't Judge A Book By Its Cover is her second book. Her first book, A Girl Like Me, was published 5 years ago. Susan also opened her own tea shop and had it for 3 years. After she closed, she started companionship with elderly folks and today works in an assisted living facility. She has always liked to write and share from her heart. Susan leads a simple spiritual life, loves to be there for others, and knows that she has a purpose here on earth. She is soft spoken but loves to carry a message of hope.